GREY WOLF'S BRAND

layla Audeamus

Brilliant Books Literary
137 Forest Park Lane Thomasville
North Carolina 27360 USA

DEDICATION

To my late Master, my life became whole when I gave myself to you. To all of my friends in the "Lifestyle;" your kink may not be my kink, but I respect your kink and love you for the things we do.

CONTENTS

CHAPTER 1

Louise Denton-Jones, or LuLu to her friends, answered the ringing phone. "Good-morning Maggie, how's London?" Lady Margaret Wattley's name had popped up on the caller ID, making the greeting possible. "When are you and Harry coming for a visit?"

Lady Margaret or Maggie, had been at university in London with LuLu and their friendship had lasted through the years. "Actually dear, Harry and I are headed your way right now. A friend of Harry's is coming with us, Jack Harris. The weather here is atrocious so we are hoping yours will be better. Can you have someone pick us up at the West Houston airport in about twelve hours?"

LuLu jotted a note for Martin, the houseman. "Will do, is Harry's friend a lifestyler? We wouldn't want to mix our visitors this weekend."

Maggie answered, "He is not only in the lifestyle, but, you've heard of the Grey Wolf, well, that's who he is."

"Mm, yes, I used to read his online-journal every day, but I thought he had dropped out? How does Harry know him?" LuLu was more than a little interested in the extra visitor.

"Don't worry, I will tell you all about it when we get in. Have to run, see you in twelve." The line went dead. That was just like Maggie, talk and run. She had been like that at school, too, always in a hurry.

LuLu put the phone down and pressed the intercom button. "Martin, please come to the office."

It had been Mark's office and still showed the manliness of his presence. LuLu's husband had passed away more than five years before and except for changing a few of the photos on the desk, the addition of an early Constable she had bought from her godparent's collection, and a smaller desk chair, the room was virtually unchanged from the day Mark last used the room.

John Edward Martin, or simply Martin, was LuLu's houseman, driver, and husband of Libby Martin, the cook/housekeeper. The house wasn't especially large by Texas standards, but it sat in a little more than twenty acres just outside of Houston, Texas. Mark had had it built when he decided it was time for them to move out of the city into the quite solitude of the country. She loved the place, it was her Mark in every timber, stone, carving, and finish.

Just after the accident that left Mark in a coma, the Martin's had been hired as a couple to care for the house, grounds, and help LuLu with Mark's care. A girl, Maria, came during the days to help with the cleaning, but the Martins lived in the apartment over the garage so someone was always close by.

Martin was retired military and still sported the close-cropped hair and erect bearing. He and Libby had never had children and after twenty-four years of service, decided the life of live-in servants fit them best. When the position with Mrs. Denton-Jones became available, it worked well for all concerned.

Martin's soft knock on the door alerted LuLu. "Ma'am?" Dressed in a dark suit, it made the slightly greying man look like any other visitor to LuLu's office. He didn't exactly stand at attention, that had been nixed the first day he came to work, but he did the closest thing that still kept him comfortable with being in the presence of his employer. "Is there something I can get you?"

LuLu took the note and handed it to him. "Lady Margaret, Harry, and a guest, Jack Harris, will be arriving at the West Houston strip at about 8:30 this evening. I want you to pick them up and bring them here. Please have Maria prepare their rooms and let Libby know there will be extra guests for the next few days. Have her stay with the regular menu; just expand it for our visitors."

Martin jotted a couple of notes on the paper she had given him. "How long will they be here? Oh, and Mr. Saxby said he would be coming with the Chairman in the morning for a meeting. Should I have the guest-house aired for him and his staff?"

"Oh dear, what does Saxby want and why is the Chairman coming?" Elliot Saxby was the head of security for the Foundation that LuLu worked for and Gordon Allen was the Chairman. A visit from either one was not unusual, but from both men together, it was not the norm.

The Foundation was headquartered in Florida and was the brainchild of Gordon Allen and LuLu. Several years ago, while Mark was still alive and working for Daniel Fields at Field Energy, LuLu had begun a conversation with Allen. He was looking for something to do with the money he had just received from the sale of his businesses and the non-profit he started had grown from LuLu's ideas. When Mark had his accident and was brought home to be cared for, the Chairman had reached out to LuLu and asked her to come to work for the firm she had helped create.

It was a winning solution for both of them. Although Mark needed round the clock care, LuLu had a nursing service that took care of those needs while she spent her time at Mark's side. The doctor's had told her he would probably never recover, but she still sat by his bedside and talked or read to him. It was her place and she would not leave his side.

When the Chairman heard about it, he insisted she needed to have something to keep her busy and he wanted her to work for the Foundation. She could work from home, and would not have to leave Mark. The Chairman had insisted she hire live-in help and he had found Martin and his wife.

"Ma'am, all Saxby said was they had to talk to you in the morning and the plane would be here by eight a.m. Shall I have Maria open the guest house?" LuLu nodded her agreement and Martin turned and left.

She liked the Chairman, but he was not a lifestyle person. Most of the people she knew, the people who had been friends with her and Mark, were "in the lifestyle."

Her hand caressed the heavy chainmail collar/necklace she wore. Mark had put it on her many years before in a formal ceremony, much like a marriage rite but only, for them, more significant. Except for a few times when she had to have it removed for medical tests, it had been around her neck. It was a part of her, just as her wedding rings and contract ring were a part of her hand. It was Mark's collar and as long as she wore it, he was still with her.

BDSM; it has several meanings. For some it is bondage, discipline, sadism, and masochism, but for others it can be dominance and submission. The people that she and Mark knew and were friends with were part of a small sub-set of BDSM known as M/s or Master/slave. Of the many branches of the "lifestyle", M/s or male Master, female slave couples were less than one percent of the whole.

Mark's boss, Daniel Fields, had been a Master and was Mark's mentor. Master Daniel had mentored several men over the years, but Mark had been his first and for LuLu, his best pupil. The home Master Daniel had shared with his slave/wife Clarisse, was less than five miles from the house Mark had built. Before Clarisse had passed away, the home she and Master Daniel had was always open and inviting for the men he had mentored and the slave/wives, they owned.

Owned, that may sound strange to some people, it had to LuLu when she first heard about it, but Mark had spent many patient months explaining what life with him would be and in the end, it was something LuLu not just welcomed, but craved. Mark had seen it in her; the need to serve, to let someone else make the decisions, to control her and give her structure in her life. She was not a doormat; this was a common misconception, but was an intelligent, well-educated woman who was dynamic and caring.

Mark was just over fifteen years older than LuLu and had been in the lifestyle for several years. He had played with several women before, but had never found the one he wanted to make his wife. Some men never found the mate that was that close to a perfect match, but when Mark saw LuLu, he just knew she was the right one. Many months, hours of talking, and some intense dating proved they were the perfect couple. They were married less than a year later, within another year and after months of contract negotiations; Mark placed his collar on her in a very moving ceremony.

Mark and LuLu were just one of the couples who were a part of the group that met at Master Daniel's house every weekend. The men he had mentored over the years numbered over thirty, but only a dozen were still in the Houston area and all were welcome when they were in town. After Master Daniel's slave/wife Clarisse passed away, he spent more and more of his time at his home, expanding and adding to his private dungeon.

About three years before his wife passed, Master Daniel had sold his business and they traveled. It wasn't long though before she was complaining of being tired all the time and a trip to the doctor proved the cause to be a cancer of the blood. For the rest of her days Master Daniel was at her side. When the end came, she was surrounded by friends and her head was resting on her Master's shoulder. He scattered her ashes over the land she loved.

Before Master Daniel followed her, he formed a trust to protect the property where his home and dungeon were located. He wanted the men he had trained to have it for play and as a place to train future Masters. It was even incorporated in the State of Texas as "**B**ig **D**an's **S**ocial **M**uster" or simply as the "Social Club." A man and his wife who were the caretakers for the property occupied a small house. The house and dungeon are still used each weekend for get-togethers and formal ceremonies. On the anniversary of Master Daniel's and slave Clarisse's birthdays, formal parties were held to mark the occasions, and toasts drunk to the founder and his slave.

Maggie and her husband, Harry, were also in the lifestyle. Harry had been a pupil of Master Daniel, but had married his slave/wife, Lady Margaret, several years before and they lived in London. Before Harry retired, he had been a very successful investment banker. LuLu guessed the reason for their trip to Houston was to perform a renewal ceremony at the Social Club. LuLu just hoped the visit of Saxby and the Chairman would not interfere with the plans she would have for Maggie and Harry.

Alice, LuLu's secretary, came in and sat in the chair across the desk from her boss. "The letters from the professor have been filed and the plans for the clinics have been uploaded into the system. Mr. Anthony called and said he had five more packages to deliver and wants to know where you want them."

LuLu thought for a moment. Mr. Anthony was an old friend from Cyprus who helped with moving people out of countries where they were no longer welcome into countries where they were. The references to "packages" were his way of saying, he had five people who were on the move, and he wanted to know where they would be going.

This was one of the projects LuLu had taken up quite by accident. Mark had been the head of Field Energy's Middle Eastern division. The offices were on the island of Cyprus and Mark and LuLu had lived there for almost eleven years. Mark was close to the various clients his company had in the area without having to live in their restrictive societies. LuLu had taught school for a few years while their son was a student and through her teaching had made several friends in the expatriate community. One of the friends was Mr. Anthony who owned several small cargo ships that moved containers from ports all around the eastern Mediterranean.

When various conflicts erupted in the area, people became refugees until the fighting ended and they could go back to their homes. The school LuLu taught in had been opened for the children of families who were unsettled by war and she made friends with their parents. The current state of war in Syria and Iraq had made life for many Orthodox Christians unbearable and the advent of the ISIS Caliphate had meant they could never go back to their homes. Several turned to LuLu for help.

She had not been in Cyprus for many years, but the friendships she and Mark had made did not end when they moved back to the United States. At first, the people had been family members of friends in the Houston area, but soon it was friends of friends. They all needed to be taken out of the war-zones, moved to places of safety, and then sent on to their final destinations. So, now Mr. Anthony had another five people needing to be taken care of. It seemed the need for help was not going to slow anytime soon.

"I will call Mr. Anthony when I have a place arranged. Please call my friend in Paris," LuLu looked up at the clock on the wall opposite her desk to check the time, "He should be back from lunch by now."

Alice got up and headed to her little office. LuLu picked up the phone and called the kitchen. Libby Martin, the cook, picked up the phone and answered LuLu. "Yes?"

"Libby, could you please send me some coffee and my breakfast? I have a lot of work to do and no time to get to the dining room."

Libby shook her head, the boss often ate at her desk or didn't eat at all. "Yes, ma'am, I'll have it brought right up, but you really need to eat more, it's not good for you to keep missing meals."

"Ok, ok, I'll try to get down for lunch. Did Martin tell you about the guests?"

"Yes, and I have put some of the Chairman's favorite foods on for lunch tomorrow. I know how much he likes my homemade bread." Libby was a wonderful cook and the Chairman was one of her favorites.

"Thank you for thinking of it, I have no idea how long he will be here, but I am sure he will stay for lunch if your bread is on the menu." LuLu put the phone down and got back to her work. So much to do…

CHAPTER 2

Maggie looked out of the small jet's window at the general aviation hangers as the plane rolled past. She saw the car with Martin standing next to it and waited for the pilot to stop before she got up to deplane. Her husband Harry was still deep in conversation with Jack and she had to remind them it was time to leave. Harry helped her with her suit bag and they all walked down the steps and thanked the pilot on their way out. Jack stayed behind to give his pilot instructions and then joined them at the car.

Harry walked up to Martin and handed him the carry-ons to put in the trunk. The co-pilot and steward from the plane were loading the luggage into the car and Martin turned to open the doors. Harry introduced Jack to Martin and the three passengers got into the back seat for the ride to LuLu's house.

Martin recognized Jack Harris. Anybody who had ever been in some kind of Special Operations was familiar with his story. Martin had spent almost 6 years as an Airborne Ranger, same as Elliott Saxby, and when he retired from the service had thought about applying to the company Harris had started a few years before. The company provided security services to private companies, individuals, and governments. Saxby had told him about the position with Mrs. Denton-Jones and after all the years he and Libby had moved from place to place, having one address for more than two years made more sense. He took the current job and was happy with his decision.

Several men he knew had applied to Harris's company, but only a few made the cut. Harris was a former Navy SEAL, but he hired from all of the Special Operations groups. Before he sold his company a few years back, it was the premier place for men with special abilities to find work that paid very well. The men that bought it, were not as particular in their hiring or in the jobs they accepted and the company's reputation was not what it had been, but Harris was no longer at its head and had no say over its future.

The drive to the house was not very long, within minutes, the door to the house was open, and LuLu was waiting to greet her guests. "Maggie! You are looking great and so is Master Harry." Margaret looked at her Master/husband for the discreet nod that would give her permission to hug her friend. Harry caught her eye and gave his assent.

In the lifestyle as they practiced it, there were protocols for social situations that Masters and slaves always observed when in the company of other lifestylers. A slave or Master did not touch another Master or their slave without permission. LuLu was Mark's widow and would behave as he had trained her, but the longstanding friendship she had with Maggie predated the slavery so for them the rules were more relaxed. LuLu hugged her friend, but only shook hands with Master Harry. He then introduced her to Master Jack.

Before the formal introductions, they all went inside out of the Texas heat. It was after nine in the evening, but the heat of the day had not fully dissipated. LuLu led them all into the living room, picked up the phone, and told Libby to have Martin bring the snacks up after he put the luggage in the rooms. Out of the corner of her eye, she looked at Jack Harris.

Master Harry had briefly introduced him before they came indoors but she wanted to get a better look at him in the light. He was over six feet, probably close to six-four and was well muscled. His suit was expertly tailored and when he took off his suit coat, the shirt showed the promised strength of his arms. He took care of himself and did not have the slightest hint of the mid-life bulge so many men his age developed. She could see where he got the "grey" in "Grey Wolf." His hair was more salt than pepper and his face was strong and handsome.

He was a presence in the room, something that was common to Masters. Master Daniel always said it was important in a Master, but the one thing that was almost impossible to train into someone that didn't come by it naturally. All of the Masters LuLu knew had it and only a few who were not ever had that same kind of presence.

LuLu put the phone down and turned to be introduced. Master Harry did the introductions and LuLu curtsied formally to Master Jack. In their lifestyle, a well-trained slave had formal protocols she followed and one of the hallmarks was her ease of movement, grace, and how she executed acts like the formal curtsy. If Mark had still been alive, he would have been proud of his slave.

Master Jack put out his hand and took hers. "I am very happy to meet you. Harry and Margaret have told me a lot about you, but they didn't tell me you were nearly this lovely." LuLu blushed. She always did when someone said anything about her looks. Mark had always glowed when anyone took the liberty of praising his wife's looks, LuLu didn't.

Mark had been very protective of her and although he would often tell her she was a "good girl" or his "lovely girl," she didn't really like for anyone to comment on how she looked. She was still, and as she felt, would always be wearing black. She was in mourning for Mark, she still wore his collar, and to her, that would never change. Subconsciously her fingers caressed the chainmail of the collar.

"I see you still wear your Master's collar. A very interesting design, I don't think I have ever seen one like it." Jack was looking at her closely, she almost felt like he could see inside her. It made her blush even deeper.

LuLu stammered, "I, uh, yes, uh, Mark, uh, my Master, designed it so I could wear it all the time. He liked chainmail and he had it made for me. He was known as "Dragon Master" so the chainmail fit his symbol." She lowered her eyes, it was difficult for her to look into his intense blue eyes.

"LuLu, may I call you LuLu?" Jack asked softly, "Please look at me. I would like to see your soft brown eyes." She raised her eyes to look at him again. She could feel the blush get deeper, but then realized, it wasn't a blush, he made her feel warm, hot even. It was unsettling to her.

Martin came in with a tray of snacks then went to the bar in the corner and made drinks for everyone. Martin was familiar with what each person drank but stopped and asked Master Jack what he would like. "Scotch, with a little ice, please."

"Right away, sir." Martin served the drinks and then left the room. LuLu moved to where Maggie was sitting on the sofa, and Jack followed. She sat in one of the wingback chairs near her friend.

"How was the flight over? We pulled a tail-wind last week and cut forty-five minutes off of the return, but I know this time of the year it is just as likely to be a head wind too." LuLu had learned how to fly several years before, but now was content to be a passenger, which did not, however, keep her from being interested in how the plane she was in was performing.

Maggie had never been into flying, for her it was just a way to get from one place to the next. "It was a bit bumpy, I am glad we had such a light breakfast." Maggie motioned to the tray table with the sandwiches Martin had brought in. "Libby makes such wonderful snacks. I didn't realize how hungry I was until Martin brought the food out."

LuLu leaned toward Maggie. "So, tell me, are you and Master Harry going to renew your contract this week? I know it is about that time."

Maggie nodded her head, "we have already called everyone and invited them to come. Harry wants to use a new brand he had made. The old one is faded enough that the one he has now will look so much better. He wasn't happy with the one he did last time."

Harry was known as the "Fox" and his symbol was a very stylized, bushy tailed fox. The brand was a part of the contract ceremony that was renewed every five years. In the Social Club's group, the Masters use a cold branding technique to mark their slaves. While others liked the hot brand that burns a permanent mark into their slave's lower back, buttocks, inner thigh, or breasts, their group used the cold brand that, although not as permanent as the hot brand, was more precise and made for a crisper image. Each of the Masters had a symbol that marked their slaves. For LuLu, it had been a dragon, for Maggie, it was the fox.

LuLu's brand had long since faded. Mark had been put into a coma by the accident and lived for more than five years afterwards, but he had been dead for these past five years. The last contract ceremony Mark had for LuLu was two years before the accident. Twelve years, had it really been that long since her Master had marked his property with his dragon brand? LuLu shook her head.

While Maggie was talking, Jack was watching LuLu and he wondered what she was thinking. His late slave/wife, Emily, had been very petit and a natural blond, the very opposite of LuLu. She was about five and a half feet tall, brown hair, mmm, uncolored, just a hint of grey in the curly hair around the edge of her very pretty face. There were a few grey, no, white, hair mixed in with the brown, just enough so it had to be natural.

She had the same grace and ease of movement that most well trained slaves of his acquaintance had shown. Jack had not known her late Master, Mark, but he and Harry had been friends for years, he respected his judgment, and Harry had told him what a great friend and mentor Mark had been to him. Harry had also told him about LuLu. Did he really want to try to take her on right now? Was he ready to move on with his life?

For almost thirty years he had lived in the lifestyle and for most of those years, Emily had been at his side. He had not been lucky enough to have a mentor like Master Daniel. His life in the military and then as a member of an elite SEAL team had left him little time to spend learning with a mentor. Most of what he knew had come from some books he was fortunate enough to find during one of his trips home on leave.

Jack had known he was different from the time he was a teenager. He didn't understand the feelings he had and unlike most people, it wasn't something that was "recognized" as being OK. It made it hard to talk about so he tried to keep his desires hidden. In college, he met a girl that helped him find something of what he was.

She was 100% counterculture of everything he was. Where he was conservative in manner and dress, she was showy and a bit of an exhibitionist. He had met her at a party one of the other guys took him to and for the first half of the evening he worried his being there would reflect badly on his Naval ROTC record. He was close to graduation and wanted the commission that would help him fulfill the obligation of the Navy paying for his education.

At the time, the Navy was a way to get a good education. Four years of college for four years of service didn't seem like a bad deal. He wanted to finish and he didn't need anything spoiling his plans, especially not a silly party in an off-campus house. One of the guys from his unit had talked him into coming and the people he was meeting were interesting, but also just a bit strange. That is where he had met Janice.

Where he was button-down collars, she was eclectic mid-century. Her tight dress reminded him of a "Betty-Boop" decal that was on one of the planes he had seen in an old war movie. She had generous curves and a full bust that he could still dream about. Before the end of the night, he didn't care that it might be hard to get her lipstick out of his shirt collar. He saw her quite often after that evening.

By the end of the first month, she wanted him to stay the night with her and the one night turned into a weekend. It was on that weekend he learned something of what he was. Janice liked to tease him. She would get up close to him, press her body into him, and when he would start to react to her, embrace her, she would move just out of his reach.

He had had sex with girls before, mostly quick flings that lasted only a few dates, but with Janice, it was more fulfilling and harder. There was something very basic and primal with Janice.

By the time he would catch her, it was more than just wanting the release of his urge, it was a wanting to possess her, make her his, to own and control her. It was the second time she did this, played the hard-to-get vamp, that when he finally caught her she told him what she wanted. "I want you to spank me. Spank me for being bad," she said.

Jack looked at her, not really knowing what she wanted him to do. "You want me to spank you?" His mind was confused. The Navy officer that was in charge of his unit at the college had played several training films on sexual harassment, rape, and when NO means NO. He had never struck a girl and didn't know if he could. "I can't do that, I can't hurt you Janice."

She pressed closer to him, "Yes you can, and I want you to spank me. Look, it's not that hard and I want you to do it, please, for me." He saw the wanting in her eyes. "Just let me lay across your knees, and use your bare hand on my ass. Take a couple of swats then I can show you from there." She laid her body across his, her short skirt almost baring her skimpily clad bottom.

It did look inviting, he held her with one arm and with his free hand, caressed her bottom. She wiggled against him and he could feel himself start to respond. The first swat was a soft smack, the second was a bit harder, and each time, he would rub her ass-cheeks with his open hand. "That's right, now you see, you can do this." Janice pulled her skirt up with her hand, Jack pulled her brief panties down far enough to have pink cheeks to smack.

His palm began to sting from the open-handed swats, but he would rub her reddening flesh after every smack and his cock was getting harder as Janice wiggled and rubbed herself into his lap. By the time she told him to take her, he had never known his cock could get that hard or he could want to have sex so badly. When it was over, Janice explained some of what had happened to him.

"I like the pain, to me, it really isn't pain, but something I need and want. And, I could tell, you like it too. Most guys can't get around the idea of not hitting a woman, but once you tried it, you really got into it." She snuggled up to him and he began to stroke her naked body while she talked. "I have a couple of friends you should meet. His name is George and her name is Tia, they are a couple, but they like for people to watch them while they play. Hey, don't look shocked, for us, this is the essence of "play.""

A few days later, Janice called and told him to meet her at the house where the party had been. He got there about 7:30 and the man that came to the door was not much older than Jack was. He introduced himself as George and invited Jack inside. The house looked a lot different without all of the people. The rooms were neat and tidy with a hint of the furniture polish used to dust with still in the air. A small woman came from the kitchen and Janice followed her. Janice introduced Tia to him.

Tia was dressed in the kind of clothing he had seen his mom wear in old pictures from the 1940s and 50s. She had longish brown hair pulled back into a ponytail, dark red lipstick, and nail polish to match. Her dress was very short and as she walked in the high-heels she was wearing, a hint of stocking tops peeked out from underneath. He also noticed the stockings were the old-fashioned kind with seams down the back.

George asked them to sit in the living room while Tia and Janice finished the preparations for dinner. When it was time to eat, Tia asked George to come to supper. The food was delicious and throughout the entire meal, Jack felt there was an unspoken communication going on between George and Tia. When George would get close to finishing his iced-tea, Tia was there to refill his glass. Anything George could have wanted; Tia had anticipated his wants and fulfilled them.

When supper finished, the girls stayed to clear things up and George invited Jack to see his playroom in the basement. It seemed important to George, but Jack didn't know what was so important or special about a playroom, after all, they were for kids, not adults. Jack suspected it was where George and his friends would watch a game on TV while the wives visited upstairs. What he showed him was a surprise.

At the bottom of the basement stairs, were three doors. One had a sign on it, "Laundry", and another sign that read "Restroom." The third door was unmarked. George saw Jack looking at the doors, "We put signs up because when we had friends over, they kept opening the laundry room door expecting to find the bathroom." George opened the third door.

It was dark inside until George reached in and flipped a light switch. The edges of the room glowed with a soft light hidden from direct view by moldings that decorated the walls high up, near the ceiling. A dimmer switch brought the lights up to a few shade lighter but then George pushed another switch that activated dozens of penlights around the ceiling. As he walked into the room, he noticed that the penlights were shining down on various pieces of strange looking furniture and structures.

George motioned him to a leather sofa that was near the center of the room. Jack sat down while George began to explain. "Welcome to our dungeon. It may seem strange to you, Janice tells me you are not familiar with our kind of lifestyle, but hopefully you will understand more before the evening is through." He walked over to a large X made from joined wood and ran his hand over the smooth surface.

"This is a Saint Andrews Cross. We use it when we play and tonight, Janice has asked me to show you how it is done." He moved a few feet away and ran his hand over a piece that looked like a strange sawhorse. "This is a spanking bench, well, my version of a spanking bench. I am also going to use this with Tia; Janice really wants you to see how this is used. She told me you had spanked her the other night and might need a few pointers on how it works best. And then, there is always the bare handed over-the-knee spanking that is a real turn-on for both the spanker and the spankee!" He chuckled and came to sit on the sofa.

Jack turned to him, "but, how? I was raised to never hit a woman and sure, it was fun what Janice had me do the other night, but, well, is it OK?" George looked into his eyes.

"Jack, up until a few years ago, what we do was considered a mental illness, but now, well, now it is understood that between consenting adults, it is alright. But it is the thing about consent that is the important part." Tia and Janice entered the room just then and Tia finished his statement.

"What we do must be safe, sane, and consensual. What George and I do together is all of that. I trust George; really trust him. A lot of people use the word trust without ever understanding what it really means. When you have a person that you can trust to take you where you want to go and know they will keep you safe and protected while pushing your limits that is a very special kind of trust. This is what I have with George."

Janice also wanted to help Jack understand. "The other night, I asked you to spank me, and for you, it was hard. I know you enjoyed it, uh, I could feel you getting bigger, but you had trouble getting around the idea that you don't hit a woman. I want George to show you what it is we do; if you are uncomfortable with what you will see, please try to wait until he finishes, and then we can go. I hope you like it, I think you will, but, uh," she looked over at George, "whenever you are ready. Do you want to start with me or Tia?"

Tia put her hand on Janice's arm, "Let me go first. He may want to uhm, uh continue with you after George's demonstration and I wouldn't want him to miss the spanking bench." She turned back to Jack, "I love the spanking bench, it's my favorite, and George built it especially for me." With that, she walked over to the bench and proceeded to remove her clothes. Janice helped hold her things as she took them off, but in seconds, she was wearing nothing but a garter belt, the stockings it held up and the high-heeled shoes.

George put a pair of leather cuffs on her wrists and explained to Jack what he was doing. "Tia likes to be restrained and blindfolded while we play on the bench." He slipped the blindfold over her eyes, fastened the cuffs to eyebolts on the bench and Tia was secured to the bench with her knees resting on separate platforms and her torso resting over a central padded beam that placed her posterior in the perfect position. The way she laid across the beam allowed her ample bare breasts to hang on each side and rub against the sides of the beam. Jack noticed her nipples were dark, large, and had clamps attached to them.

Janice sat with Jack while George picked up a small towel to dry his hands. When George turned back to Tia, he rubbed her bare buttocks with both of his hands. He caressed her thighs and then moved to the inner thighs and up to her pubic area. In the background, music started to play very softly. The beat of the tune would be the rhythm of what was to come. George leaned down and whispered in Tia's ear, he continued to caress her, then gave her a very loud slap on her left butt cheek.

Tia stiffened slightly then relaxed as George caressed her where his hand had hit. The next slap came on the downbeat and Jack recognized the action in front of him was being played to the music that filled the air. Tia no longer stiffened, but instead was pushing toward George's hand with each stroke he took. For several minutes he continued then leaned over and whispered to Tia again.

He reached for something from the table next to him and Janice whispered in Jack's ear that it was called a flogger. George laid the flogger on Tia's back and gently ran it up and down her body before pulling it back and bringing it down on her red ass-cheeks. The flogger had a soft sound to it and it made Tia wiggle each time he hit her with it. For several minutes George played the flogger up and down her body but as much force as he used to hit her, she tried to rise to meet the blows. The next time George leaned in to whisper to Tia, Jack looked to see what he would use on her next.

This time, George picked up a riding crop, much like the one Jack had used when he was taught to ride as a young man. George made a few practice swings in the air and the sound of the crop cutting through it could be heard over the sound of the music. Jack saw Tia stiffen a bit, but George was caressing her body with his hand and with the crop. Now George was getting more intimate with his caresses and did not stop at the pubic area, but Jack saw him part the lips of Tia's shaved pussy and caress her clit. With one finger, George entered her then put the finger in his mouth to "taste her.

George again whispered to Tia and began to tap the crop up and down her back, legs, and buttocks. Each time the tap became a little harder and then he started to use the crop on her more private parts. For the first time, he used the crop to tap her breasts and this made Tia begin to writhe on the bench. When George went back to concentrating on her inner thighs and pussy-lips, the music was beginning to swell and it was as if Tia was going with it. As the music built, Jack could sense the quickening in Tia and George.

George pressed up against the side of the bench and used his one hand to tap the crop on Tia's labia and with the other hand he reached down and pulled the nipple clip off of Tia's nipple. A loud groan came from Tia and when he moved to the other side to remove the other clip, she cried out in pleasure. "Please may I?" she begged.

George kept the rhythm going with the crop and again leaned down to whisper into her ear, but this time she cried louder, "Please let me cum, oh please!"

With a few last strikes of the crop George growled at her, "Cum for me, cum now!" Tia contorted and Jack understood why he restrained her. If she had not been, she could have hurt herself as she orgasmed. George laid the riding crop aside and took a light blanket from the table. He opened it and put it over Tia, then undid her restraints. He wrapped her in his arms and helped her to a small sofa near Jack and Janice.

George removed the blindfold and for the first time Jack could see the look on Tia's face. She was glowing in the aftermath of the orgasm and the spanking George had given her. The smile on her said it all, she was happy indeed.

Janice looked at Jack, "Do you think you can learn to do that for me? This is what I like Jack Harris and I can tell by your pants, you enjoyed it too." Jack blushed at the reference to his rising cock, but before he could retort, she had kissed him and taken George's proffered hand. "Now it is my turn. When we finish, you can tell me, or better yet, show me how you like it." With that she started to disrobe.

Jack had never been around people that were so casual about removing their clothes, but first Tia and then Janice did it without thinking. Now, Janice stood before him wearing nothing but the shoes she had worn to dinner. She walked over to the cross thing and George put a pair of leather cuffs on each wrist and ankle. He restrained each wrist to an upper part of the X and then spread her legs to attach each ankle to one of the lower parts. With her back to him she made a lovely target for George. As he put the blindfold on her, she told Jack that part of the joy of using the blindfold was the "anticipation and not knowing what exactly was coming."

The music had changed to a different ambient sound, one that reminded him of something he had heard long ago. George would again use the music as a measure of the tempo he would use when he "played" with Janice. Before George could get started, Tia, wrapped in the blanket, came to sit near Jack and sip from a cold bottle of water. With a nod from Tia, George got started.

For the first few moments, the only thing George did was walk around Janice, his leather boots just slightly louder than the music playing in the background. Jack recognized what George was doing, he was pacing, letting her know he was there, but not interacting with her just yet, building up her anticipation of what was to come. Then George leaned in and without touching her, whispered in Janice's ear. Jack saw her stiffen and wondered what George had said, he would have to remember to ask her later.

Finally, George reached over and picked up the same soft flogger that he had used on Tia…

Jack heard his name called a couple of times, but it wasn't until Harry tapped him on the shoulder that he emerged from his reverie. He blinked and looked around the room. It took a second to remember where he was. "Look old man," Harry teased, "Maggie and I should be the ones with jet lag, not you. Welcome back to us."

Jack looked over at LuLu and wondered if she was the one that triggered the old memories of Janice. He smiled and apologized for letting his mind wander. "It seems the older I get, the more places my mind finds to go, sorry about that. Maybe it is time to turn in."

LuLu pushed the hidden button next to her chair and Martin came in. "Martin, please show Mr. Harris to his room." She turned to Maggie, "I know you two can find your room, it's the same every time you visit.

She offered her hand to Jack, "It has been nice meeting you, I hope you have a good night's sleep. Martin will see to your needs." A peck on the check for Maggie and LuLu was out of the room.

Once the visitors were in their respective rooms, she took the stairs up to hers. Visitors were on the left of the stairs-case and her master suite was on the right. It was where she felt closest to her late husband.

Mark had spent many years working for Field Energy and his primary means for relaxation was woodworking. He had made several pieces of furniture for their private dungeons and when this house was built he chose the specific woods that would be used for moldings, trims, and cabinets. The result was a one-of-a-kind masterpiece that would never be built again. In her private room, the work was very evident.

The fireplace and sitting area were not the special part, the double walk-in closets were pretty normal for a house this size, the large double bathrooms and separate dressing rooms were not even that unique, no it was the wardrobes that held the secrets to this room. When first entering the room it was normal to have doors leading off into other rooms like closets or bathrooms, but in this room, only the main door was apparent. One way in, one way out. Two very ornate wardrobes graced the walls, but no other doors.

Open one of the wardrobes, the one on the left, and the door to the bathrooms, dressing rooms, and closets was revealed. Mark had carefully hidden them within the wardrobes and the inside of the doors of the wardrobes had mirrors that made last minute checks of attire easier. The second wardrobe was always kept locked and only one other person held the key, Martin.

The second wardrobe had two secrets. The interior of the wardrobe was her jewelry cabinet and was connected to an alarm system that was state-of-the-art. Armed people would surround anyone who tried to open that door without the proper key before they could ever manage to get the door open. But, in the back of the jewelry cabinet, a second secret was hidden. A hook in the rear could be turned and the whole cabinet would swing away from the wall and this led the way to the most private of privates.

It was a mini-dungeon. Mark had built a large, well outfitted dungeon on the top floor that several visitors had seen and used while Mark was alive, but it was reached by an elevator specially built into the house when it was being constructed. No, Mark had put this private space in the house when it was designed and over time, had finished it to suit his wants and needs.

Mark made all of the furniture in this private space and the finish work had all been his. He had completed it for LuLu's birthday just months before the accident. They had never gotten to use it as much as she had hoped for when he gave it to her. Now, she liked to sit inside and remember her lost Master and just how lonely she really was.

CHAPTER 3

Her London visitors were still living on GMT and everyone else in the household were former military and used to getting up early. LuLu was dressed and down for breakfast before the sun was up and was not surprised when she found the rest of her guests ready for a cup of coffee. Libby had set the machine up in anticipation of early risers and the first pot of coffee was ready.

LuLu could smell the bread Libby was baking and remembered the Chairman and Saxby were due in very soon. Martin was busy serving coffee and she reminded him he had people to get from the airport. "The pilot will have ground control call when they get close enough for me to leave." LuLu was happy she had such an efficient staff to look after things.

Maggie and Harry were planning on going to the Galleria for some shopping and Martin had given them the keys to one of the cars. They would leave just after breakfast, but before the other visitors arrived. Jack wanted to check in with his people in Colorado before they left for the day. LuLu finished her breakfast and headed to her office.

Just before eight the phone on her desk buzzed, the Chairman and Saxby were here. LuLu walked out to the foyer to greet them just as she saw Saxby and Jack Harris shaking hands. Saxby was introducing Harris to the Chairman as she walked up. The Chairman leaned over and gave LuLu a peck on the cheek and she shook Saxby's hand. She still didn't know what the business was they were here for.

Saxby looked at the Chairman, "Sir, this guy," motioning to Jack, "is one of the best in the business; we should have him in on this."

The Chairman looked at Jack and took his hand, "Will you help us with a little problem we may have Mr. Harris?"

Jack countered, "If you promise to call me Jack, sure, I'll put my two cents in, if it means anything."

Saxby looked at Jack, "Seriously, this is just your thing. And I would trust your two cents any day."

They all walked into the office and sat around the conference table that was at the other end of the room. Martin started to leave and the Chairman stopped him. "Ask someone else to bring us coffee, you need to be here also." Martin looked to LuLu and she nodded. He went to the desk and asked Libby to send Maria up with coffee for the group.

When they were all seated and Maria had left the cart with the coffee service, Saxby stood up and started his presentation. He put a thumb drive in the flat-screen on the wall at the end of the table and a picture of LuLu walking up some stairs to a house came on the screen. "Ma'am, can you tell me when and where this was taken?"

All eyes turned to LuLu. "It was taken almost two weeks ago in London. That is the front door to my godparent's house in Wilton Street just off Upper Belgravia Square." The next picture flashed onto the screen, "That is the same house, but this time I am coming out of the door." She looked over at Saxby to try to understand what the meaning of all of this was, but then the next photo appeared on the screen. "Uh, that is outside of the boot-makers in Knightsbridge. I've had boots made there since my college days and Mark used to get his made there as well. What is all of this about?"

Saxby turned back to the group. "These photos were found on a thumb-drive in London. The British police picked up a man who they have been following for several months. He is connected to a group that recruits British nationals to be ISIS fighters in Syria and Iraq. When he was taken, this was found in his house, and the boys at MI5 could not identify all of the people in the pictures. These were in a group of photos transmitted to the CIA for identification and one of the men there recognized your picture. He called me in and wanted to know why you were part of a collection kept by a terrorist group."

Saxby went on, "I told him you had been in London within the last few weeks, but he asked me to check it out just the same. Now that has been done, we have a bigger problem. Why do they want your picture and what do they plan on doing with it?" He sat down and waited for the information to sink in.

The Chairman was the first to speak. "What were you doing in London anyway?"

LuLu shifted in her chair, "My godparents have sold their home in London and are moving out to the country, to Kent. The London house has been in the family since the late 18th century and is the last of the large possessions they own. Over the years, I have tried to help them, but the taxes just keep eating everything, first it was Mickleham Hall in the 1960s, then it was many of the paintings and some furniture, and now it is the London house. I offered to buy it from them, but they wouldn't hear of it. Most of the furniture I have in my different houses comes from either Mickleham Hall or the London house and the few pieces they are taking to Kent I have already purchased so it will come to me once they are gone. While I was there this last time, I did buy the car, and it should be arriving by boat sometime in the next week." She motioned to the silver coffee service, "The coffee service was also one of my purchases. I just hated to see everything go for nothing."

It was then that Saxby spoke what was on his mind. "Ma'am, I think they have you on a hit list of some kind. I don't know what you have done that might make them mad at you, but one picture might be a mistake, two, mmm, maybe just trying to make sure it is really not the person they are looking for, but three, that tells me you are on somebody's radar. Any idea what may be the reason for this kind of attention?"

Martin looked at LuLu, "Could they have something to do with the packages you help get delivered?" LuLu blushed, she hadn't thought about that. Jack picked up on the flash of emotion and started to ask but the Chairman jumped in first.

"Packages?, packages?, what does he mean by packages?" The Chairman tried to hide his concern for his friend with a tinge of anger. "Explain to me what he means by 'Packages!'."

LuLu turned her attention toward the Chairman. "Packages mean people. For almost three years I have been helping Orthodox Christians and some other "unwelcome" people leave Syria, Lebanon, Iraq, and now the new Caliphate that ISIS has declared." For the next ten minutes she told them the whole story. Nothing was hidden from this group of men who were concerned for her safety. She told them who Mr. Anthony was, were the people came from, where they went, and how they got in touch with the people who brought them out.

When she finished, the Chairman had one last question for her, "How many, 'packages' have you moved?"

LuLu looked at him, "just over a hundred people."

He looked at her in shock, "My god, you have been running your own underground railroad! I'm proud of you dear, but now I'm afraid you have stuck your head up once too often and somebody wants to take it off!" Gordon Allen was part black, the great-great grandson of slaves so the reference to the Underground Railroad had a special meaning to him.

He turned to Martin, "Why wasn't I told of this?"

LuLu came to Martin's defense, "Gordon, don't take it out on Martin, he had nothing to do with this, I am the one that started it. It was just people who wanted to get family out and then friends of friends, I didn't think it was a problem. But please, please, don't blame my staff for this. If anybody it to blame it is the sick freaks that throw children off mountains and force women and girls to convert and marry their soldiers."

LuLu did not get angry often, actually, there were very few people old enough to remember when she had last lost her temper to the point of getting really mad, but she was near that now. Jack watched her and the interaction in the room, she wasn't the weak little widow Maggie and Harry thought she was, there was still plenty of fight left in her. However, now it was time for him to jump in but before he could take the floor, Saxby had a possible solution.

"Chairman, ma'am, I have a man, Arthur Millbury, former Ranger, would make a very good personal bodyguard for you. He can be here in hours and will stay on the job for as long as it takes. I have known him for several years and he's just the man for the job." Saxby knew never to come to a meeting with a problem without trying to have a readymade solution.

Jack had gotten to his feet before he realized what he was doing. "I can do it, uh, look, I'm retired, and there is nothing for me to do but bum around visiting a bunch of places that really don't interest me. If

LuLu will let me, I can look after her for as long as it takes to find the threat and neutralize it."

LuLu looked at him, well thank you, I think, but out loud she was a little more circumspect. "Mr. Harris, I am sure we couldn't possibly take you away from your retirement and Saxby, thank you for thinking of me, but really, Martin is here and that is all I need." Everybody started talking at once. Jack looked at LuLu with a hurt look on his face, the Chairman was accepting Jack's offer, and Saxby was making one last plea for Millbury. By the time the dust settled Jack was giving his word to the Chairman to look after LuLu with his life and Saxby was forced to accept that he had recommended Jack be in on the meeting to begin with, so how could he possibly object.

Martin kept his own counsel but was happy that Harris was going to be staying and helping to look after his employer. LuLu just felt as if things had been taken out of her hands and someone would tell her what they wanted her to know. Now, when Jack looked at her, she was the one with the hurt look, at least until she thought to cover it with a smile.

LuLu excused herself and left the planning to the professionals in the room. No sooner had she stepped out than the Chairman followed. "Well my girl, you are surprising. I never expected to find this kind of thing going on in my own organization, but, hmm, I guess there are always more things to life than we expect. Look, I understand your need to help people, part of what makes you the person you are is your drive to be needed and useful, but really, you could have let some of us in on this. Is it still active?"

For the first time since the morning's meeting started she was feeling like she might have done something right. "I got word that five more people were coming out yesterday. A contact of mine in Paris was going to make the arrangements to take them to France and then help them go where they wanted. Many of them have family in either Europe, North America, or Australia. A few have ties to South America, but right now it is harder to get in to some of the countries. Too many are not the best places to bring up families."

The Chairman put his arm around her shoulders. "Don't let the bad guys get to you, we can figure out a way to keep you safe. Young Harris,

Jack, has a good head on him and he has some first rate ideas. Let him take care of you and I think he will do a wonderful job of it."

They were in the living room, facing the large fireplace. The Chairman's eyes went to the mantle where a large oil painting of LuLu and Mark, done just a year before the accident, was hanging. "You still miss him, don't you girl? Look, time moves on, your son has told you this, I have tried to get you to see it, and your friends know it is time for you to come back to the land of the living. Perhaps these problems might not be problems if you weren't preoccupied with Mark's passing. Try to come back to us, you just might find life is still worth living."

The meeting was breaking up, Martin was showing Jack where the security closet was, and Saxby came to stand near the Chairman. LuLu wanted the Chairman to stay for lunch. "Gordon, Libby has been baking bread since early this morning so you must stay for lunch. I also know she has a couple more of your favorites on the menu, too."

The Chairman nodded and they went into LuLu's office. Alice came in with the messages and the Chairman and Saxby sat on the sofa near LuLu's desk. Most of the messages would be handled later, right now, she wanted to hear Saxby's version of the plan.

Saxby wasted no time in doing his briefing. "Jack Harris has offered to stay and keep Ma'am safe. He also still has some contacts in MI5, the CIA, and over at the Pentagon so he will be able to stay on top of any developments on the other end. Martin is giving him a full rundown on the security setup here. We discussed the idea and think it might be wise for you to go to the beach house. I know it would take some time for your staff to get over there and prepare the house for you, but it is something to think about. Also, if we need to, there is always the ranch, but Harris thinks that might not be a good thing to do, he said if it comes to that, it would be better to take you someplace not previously associated with you. We can look at this if or when it may be necessary, but right now, I tend to agree it would be a good thing for you to go to the beach."

LuLu sat and listened to what people had decided for her. One of her first thoughts was to go to the beach house or the ranch, but Maggie and Harry were here for their renewal ceremony and nothing was going to upset those plans, at least she hoped not. She thought for a few moments then picked up the phone. "Alice, please come in here."

In a few seconds, Alice was standing next to her desk. LuLu started giving her directions. "Call the beach house and tell Jerry to open it up, we will be there by next Wednesday. Then, let Libby and Martin know that we are making the trip, but I will follow a couple of days after them. I am going to New York for a few days and that will give them time to prepare everything. The rest of the arrangements can be made later." Alice closed her pad and left to start things moving.

The Chairman motioned for Saxby to go take a stroll around the house. When they were alone, he gave her his advice. "I think a trip to the beach is just fine, but I doubt a side trip to New York is the best thing right now. Have you thought about being without a bodyguard or Martin there to watch over you? Maybe Harris will go with you and look out for your, come to think of it, that is really quite a good idea." Before she could stop his train of thought or interject, he was on his feet and out the door. All LuLu could do was go after him.

Martin and Jack had just finished looking at the security equipment and were standing outside the office door. "Jack, can I ask you something?" said the Chairman. "LuLu is going over to the beach house about the middle of next week but while it is being made ready she wants to go to New York for a couple of days. Do you think I can get you to go with her, I mean, if you have other plans, we understand, but…" before the Chairman could finish his request Jack was nodding his agreement. "Fine, young man, fine this is going to really help us out." The Chairman literally beamed with Jack's promise to look after LuLu.

Before LuLu could say anything, Martin came to tell them lunch was being served. Jack took her by the elbow and steered her into the dining room. LuLu asked Martin to call Saxby in to eat, but he was on the phone with the security equipment firm and asked to be excused. That left just the three of them to eat and LuLu spent most of the meal listening to the Chairman and Jack talk about their respective military experiences. Once the meal was finished, the Chairman went to the kitchen to gives his thanks to Libby for the lovely meal and again remind Martin what a wonderful gem he was married too.

LuLu and Jack were left alone for the first time. It was a little awkward, she didn't like being alone with men she didn't know or wasn't related to in some way. It was up to Jack to break the ice. "LuLu, do you mind if I ask you a question? Uh, it may be kind of personal and if you don't want to answer, I will understand."

LuLu looked across the table at him, "It's alright, ask me what you want."

Jack shifted uncomfortably in the chair, "I have heard Harry and Maggie, you, and other people refer to your late husband Mark and an accident. What was the accident he had that left him in a coma?" Almost as soon as he asked the question, he regretted it, but he really wanted to know before he went any further. The pain in LuLu's eyes almost made him want to take the question back.

Voice filled with emotion, LuLu started to speak. "It's alright to ask, it's just, it's still painful to talk about. Hmm, but, here goes."

"One evening, Mark and I went to the Social Club like we did on most weekends. Master Daniel had lost his wife the spring before and we always tried to be there on the weekends for him. Mark liked to make furniture as a means of relaxation and he had just delivered a new piece of equipment to the Club's dungeon." LuLu took a sip of her coffee and went on.

"Mark almost never played with me in public; he liked to keep what we did private because his play usually finished with him using me for sex. But, he had told me that morning he wanted to show the group the new piece and was going to use me in public that evening to demonstrate the new furniture. I was looking forward to the demo, the play, being out with my Master/husband, everything."

"That night we had a wonderful dinner, good conversation, and about eleven we all walked over to the dungeon. Mark had asked me if I had something for a headache, but by the time I found him something, he told me it had gone away and he didn't need it. It was unusual, but I didn't think anything more about it."

"One of the other couples wanted to start off the evening and Mark told them to go ahead, he wanted time to get prepared. While the other people were playing, Mark put his toys out and I got ready to be suspended by a chain with a stocks and spreader bar. Mark put the leather cuffs on my wrists and ankles and the blindfold on. He secured me in the stocks and spread my legs apart with the spreader bar."

"The session began as usual, he would always pace around me, whisper in my ear, tell me what he was doing, getting me mentally prepared to take me where he wanted to go. All of that was usual. In all of the years, he had done about the same as he was doing that night. He started out using a flogger and then put it down and took a riding crop."

"The people who go to the Social Club, the men that Master Daniel had trained, all were close friends and they all knew how the other men treated their slaves. I think everybody at the demo that night knew that Mark would never use a cane on me in play because he only used that when he wanted to punish me."

LuLu took another drink from her cup, cleared her throat, and plowed ahead. "Usually when he would change from one toy to another, he would caress me, whisper to me, tell me how I was doing or what he wanted to do next, but this time, I could hear him try to speak but he was being drowned out by the music that was playing. That was the first sign something was not right, but I was blindfolded and didn't understand exactly how much trouble he was in. He put the crop down and picked up one of the small, whip like canes he rarely used. It wasn't very heavy, but it could really hurt when used with enough force and it was thin enough it did not take much to give it that force."

"Everyone who was watching thought it was part of the session and no one would ever interfere when a couple was sessioning. Something terrible was happening with Mark and no one knew it or understood what it was. He kept hitting me and hitting me. There was no rhythm to it, no nothing, it was like a punishment but I didn't know what it was I had done wrong. I took it as long as I could and then, for the first time ever, I safe-worded him, but he didn't stop, he just kept hitting me. Then I started screaming and Master Daniel decided it was time to step in."

"Whatever was happening to Mark, that stopped him and he looked at what he had done. He threw the cane down on the floor, ran out of the dungeon, and got in the car. He left me hanging there, blood running down my back where he had cut me. A couple of the other slaves put a blanket over me and one of the other Masters took me down, I don't even know which one, I had passed out by that time."

"One of the Masters that had not come that night was a doctor that was on call at the hospital that evening. He never joined us on the nights he was on call, but Master Daniel called him and Master "Bones" told him to bring me into the emergency room where he was on duty. As Master Daniel drove me to the hospital, he passed the car Mark had been driving. A fire department EMT unit had just arrived and Master Daniel stopped long enough to tell the rescue people who Mark was and where to take him."

"Later, they told me he had been able to pull off the road, but could not stop before hitting a guardrail. While he was playing with me in the dungeon he had been having several neural "misfires" that sent him out of control and they climaxed in a massive stroke in the car. He didn't know what he was doing and no one knew just how much trouble he was in. The doctor Master Daniel had look at me cleaned and bandaged my cuts then one of the girls brought me something to wear so I could stay at the hospital with Mark."

"Mark never woke up. He didn't die, they got medicine into him before that happened, but the stroke coupled with the damage from the car hitting the guard-rail, well, it was just too much. He had been in very good health before this happened so when he slipped into a coma I expected him to recover. They told me he wouldn't, but my grandmother had suffered a major stroke when I was a child and she recovered, medicine had advanced since the 1960s so they had to have something to make him better. That was not how it went."

"I brought him home, here, to the house he built for us, and I sat with him, read to him, talked to him, I did everything I could, but he never woke up. For more than five years I waited with him, but it didn't happen. I just wanted to let him know how sorry I was that I safe-worded him. Finally, a lung infection killed him." LuLu brushed a tear away before she went on.

"Maybe if I hadn't done that, safe-worded, he wouldn't have run out of the house and someone could have gotten him help before the massive stroke he had in the car. I don't know, but it has been with me since the night it happened. It has been with me since it happened and I just can't let it go."

Jack wanted to reach out to her but knew it would not have been right. He understood some of the demons that were punishing her. Trust was so important and Mark had, on the surface at least, broken that trust with LuLu. It didn't help that it was later found that he had been sick. LuLu was probably mad at him until she took on the guilt of feeling she was somehow responsible for her Master's coma. This girl had a load of baggage she was carrying and now it was up to him to decide if she was worth what it would take to bring her back.

LuLu looked over at Jack. He must think she was awful to have caused her Master such distress that it would turn into a stroke, but to her surprise, he simply smiled at her. "LuLu, I am sure you have been told this over and over again, you are not responsible for what happened to Mark. Any of us could have a stroke or heart attack in our sleep without any stress, you did not cause this, so please, let's move on and look forward to the re-commitment ceremony for Harry and Maggie."

LuLu looked down at her hands. Yep, there it was, the same answer the doctors all gave her and anyone else who knew the story. She had nothing to feel guilty about, but they just didn't understand how hard it was on her. Losing a husband was one thing, but losing her Master, well, that was so much more.

Lunch was over and it was time to get back to the office, but Jack stopped her with another few questions.

"Do you have to go just yet?" He watched her think about it and then nod her head.

"No, I guess I can stay for another few minutes." She took her seat and Jack poured more coffee for himself.

"LuLu, when is the last time you played with anyone?" Well, that was a direct question. She hadn't seen that one coming. Not even Maggie had gotten up the courage to ask her that.

Oh, what the heck, he was going to be at her side for the next few days, at least until they found out what the pictures were doing on that creeps thumb-drive in London. "Jack, the last time I played with anyone was the night my husband had his massive stroke. I don't play with people and people don't play with me." Polite be damned! Before Jack could react she was out of her chair and nearly collided with the Chairman as he returned from the kitchen. Before he could say anything to her, she was out the door.

The Chairman looked at Jack, "What happened while I was gone, is she mad at you?"

Jack took another sip of his coffee. Carefully he put the cup down, wiped his mouth on the napkin, and stood to leave the room. In a quiet but commanding voice he said, "Sir, there is nothing here that persistence and determination will not cure. Enjoy your trip back to Florida."

CHAPTER 4

Late in the afternoon Maggie and Harry returned from their shopping trip in Houston. Lady Margaret had been like so many titled English that were rich in titles but poor in the money to keep their way of living going. She had been married to another man when she was in her third year of university, but in less than a year he finished squandering what little her father had been able to leave her. Within a couple of years, she was the widow of Sir Michel Charlton of Kelsterton Priory.

He had done one of the only noble things he could in life, he left her with enough to bury him and young enough to have a chance at a better match. The Priory had to be sold to pay the death duties and Lady Margaret put the London house on the market, also. She was prepared to move into smaller lodgings if it gave her enough time to finish her university and get a job that paid enough for her to live on.

Not long after the London house had gone on the books for sale, the agent called her with a hot prospect; the agent had to be out of town and wanted to know if Lady Margaret would mind showing the house. She told her the man was only in London for a few days and he certainly had the money to buy the house. Maggie agreed.

When he came to the door, he hadn't been told the owner would be showing him the property. Thinking the woman who answered the door was the agent, he immediately started to find fault with the home. There was some work that would have to be done, she knew that, but the way this American was going on, it was a wonder the place hadn't come down around them long ago, killing them all!

Lady Margaret put up with it with the one idea front in her mind, the fact this boorish American had the money to buy the place, and she had to sell. It sustained her through most of the encounter until she took him into the morning room. On the wall was a picture of her grandfather as a young man, painted in the late 1800s by a little know artist, and which really was quite awful, but not as much as this Yank made it out to be. She had loved her grandfather and when the American said he looked like a horse-thief, that was the last straw. She whirled around on him and was ready to give him a piece of her mind, but there he stood, a silly grin on his face.

For a moment she thought he was mad, crazy, bonkers, but then he started laughing and she stamped her foot at him. "How dare you insult my, my grandfather like that." It just made him laugh the harder.

"I wondered how long it was going to take you to lose your temper, your Ladyship!" Now he guffawed at her anger.

"But, but when, how did you know it was me or that I was the owner of the house." She asked him, her anger quickly slipping away. It was pretty funny, that picture did make him look like a rogue, but horse-thief, she couldn't see it.

"Ma'am, if you don't want anyone to know who you are, don't put your picture in the main entry hall." He saw the puzzled look on her face.

"But, my picture is not in the foyer, mine is, oh, no, that isn't me, that is the horse-thief's wife." When she realized what she had said, it was funny to her also. Before long they had both had a laugh on poor old grandfather.

"Look, I need to tell you, the house really is nice, but I am not in the market to buy a house. I am a friend of Mark and LuLu. I think you went to school with LuLu and she asked me to drop in the next time I was in London." He saw the lost look on her face.

Lady Margaret started to cry. Poor Harry didn't quite know how to handle a crying woman so he just sat there and when it looked like she needed it, he offered her his handkerchief. "Look, I am sorry if I have upset you, but that really wasn't my intention."

It was then Maggie told him what was wrong and about the apparent mix-up. They had just gotten past the part about the need to sell the house and onto the introductions of first names when the doorbell rang. Maggie was still in a bit of a state and Harry offered to go to the door. She nodded her assent and sent him off and then remembered it could be the real buyer, here to look at the house. She went after Harry and found him with a red-faced man berating him at the door. "What do you mean the house is no longer on the market? That agent promised me it was still for sale and it has the sign in the window."

Before Maggie could stop him, he told the man it was no longer for sale. He closed the door and turned to find a furious Maggie about to nail him to the floor with words. Harry calmly reached for the "For Sale" card that the realtor had put in the window and tore it up. "Now, how much did you say this house will cost me?"

In three days, the sale was complete and within a year, LuLu and Mark were invited to the wedding. Six months later they were in Houston at the Social Club for a collaring ceremony, the contract signing, and the first branding.

When poor or we should say "poorer" Harry got the last of the packages from the car, he went up to the room to find his wife asking to join LuLu in her bedchamber. "Master, may I spend some time with LuLu before we have to dress for dinner?"

He knew the girls hadn't really visited much since they'd arrived and he nodded his assent. His lovely slave blew him a kiss and disappeared into LuLu's room.

Her old school friend had just put the phone down when she came in. "I've ordered some tea to be brought up, still like Earl Grey's?" LuLu asked her. They both had drunk enough of that during their college days and she still had a cup in the afternoon if at all possible. LuLu motioned Maggie to one of the chairs by the cold fireplace.

Maggie had been looking at the beautifully carved mantelpiece Mark had bought from an old house in New York. The thing had had to be stripped of multiple coats of paint and refinished, but the outcome was really quite stunning. Above it hung a picture of LuLu he had commissioned when she was about thirty. She looked so happy and the look in her eyes had been captured perfectly. Would any of them ever be able to bring back such happy, tender looks again?

LuLu studied her friend; the red in her hair was softening with the addition of more grey, just like her brown was, but the green in her eyes was still as emerald as ever. When she was younger, Maggie had the temper to go with the hair and eye color, but no more. The years with

Harry and the submission LuLu knew that Maggie had made to him, had mellowed her. She still had the energy and zest for life that had drawn them together as friends so many years ago, and regular visits with each other was a tonic for both of them.

"LuLu, the room is as pretty as always, you haven't changed a thing." Maggie sat down as the girl with the tea came in with the cart. "So, what do you think of Jack?" Maggie never did beat around the bush about anything.

LuLu thought for a moment, "I haven't really thought about him. I know he is supposed to be a wiz at security matters and protection, but that is about all. Until he quit writing it, I used to follow his journal on the web, but since it stopped, he hasn't really been in my thoughts at all. Some of what he wrote about his wife's, uh, illness and death, uh, kind of helped me when Mark was sick, but, well, then he dropped out and I didn't hear any more about him."

"He has been a friend of Harry's for years," Maggie said. "He met him when he was in the service and then a few years ago, Harry asked him to upgrade the security or lack of security system at the house in town. He stayed with us for about two weeks then, while the system was being put in and the three of us had a blast." She held her cup out and let LuLu put a sugar cube in it.

Maggie continued. "You read about his wife. Tragic one that was. He and Emily were really very close and both had found their way to each other and together in the lifestyle. She also helped when he was injured just after the Gulf War and, when he took his early retirement and started the business, she was there every step of the way. Harry thinks that is probably why he sold up and left everything in California. The business, their home, all of it, just had too much of his late wife in it for him to go on without her."

"I know he may seem like he is strong, but he really grieved for her," Maggie said. "We were both relieved when he bought the place in Telluride, but he doesn't spend much time there. He still seems a little lost."

LuLu put her cup down. She didn't know how much she could share with Maggie, they didn't have any secrets between them, but she also didn't want to cause her friend worry. "The meeting I had with the Chairman this morning," Maggie nodded to LuLu as she continued, "Well, they want me to have a little extra security for a while. The head of security for the Foundation invited Jack to the meeting and he has agreed to kind of watch over me for the next few days. Uh, I'm not sure what he will be expected to do, but after your renewal I am going to the beach house. I want to go to New York for a few days while they prepare the house and uh, well, Jack agreed to go to New York with me." Hmm, when she said it like that, it didn't even make much sense to LuLu!

Maggie beamed, "That is fantastic, two lost souls doing New York together!" She caught LuLu's shocked expression. "O LuLu, not that, no, I didn't mean that, but well, you can at least have dinner with him while you're both there and it wouldn't hurt for the two of you to just sit and talk to each other."

"I know you are still grieving for Mark, and more importantly, so does Jack. Harry spent a lot of time telling him about you and Mark, I'm sure Jack will respect your, well you know, your widowhood." Now it was Maggie's turn to blush.

LuLu felt it was time to change the subject. "So tell me, is anything special being done for your renewal or is it much like the last one?"

Maggie was always happy to talk about other things and her renewal ceremony was at the top of her list. "This time Jack is going to read the contract for us. We haven't made any changes to it, we just want to sign it, Harry will put the new brand on me, and he wants to add another ring to my labia rings. This is our fourth renewal ceremony and he wants me to have a gold ring added each time we renew."

"By the time we get to be old and grey, I shall have quite a collection of labia rings to pull my pussy lips down with!" The two girls both laughed at the mental picture Maggie's statement had conjured for them. "Oh, stop, but it is funny. Anyway, uh, I want you to stand with me like the last time, but this year I have a new robe for you, I'll bring it in before we go down to dinner."

She went on, "I am so tired of the black ones we always have to wear, this time I wanted to have you in a green robe and my robe is a nice creamy beige chiffon. Harry really likes it so that is what I am wearing. He and Jack will both be in their best leather kit."

LuLu remembered her last renewal ceremony with Mark resplendent in his best leather boots, jacket, vest, and trousers. He was so handsome that day and the ceremony so moving. She would never have another one, but she really wanted to enjoy the one her best friend was going to have. "Alright, I can do green. Anything else I need to know about it?"

Maggie thought for a moment while she finished her tea. "Not that I can think of. Doctor "Bones" is bringing his new girl but everyone else is either coming with their own Master or slave or have not RSVP'd."

"Master Bones, I haven't seen him for a couple of years. You know he was the doctor that took care of me after Mark had the accident? Well, about a year after Mark passed away I was at the Social Club for Master Daniel's ceremonial birthday party and Doc Bones was there. He was telling me how sorry he was about Mark but at the same time, telling me to get on with life, maybe even find another Master. Gee, he gave me the impression he was wanting me to consider him, but I just can't see me in a Ploy house."

Maggie was interested in that little tidbit of news, she hadn't heard about him approaching LuLu concerning accepting him as a Master. She knew LuLu would have offers, a widowed slave was usually given time to grieve over her loss, but then slave-less Masters would seek them out about accepting them as a new Master. It usually happened at social events or lifestyle gatherings but it was the normal way the community had of looking after their own.

A slave who had had the same Master for more than a few years was both a blessing and could just as well be a curse. The fact they had been with one person showed they had the capacity for loyalty and commitment, but if they were like LuLu, the bond could have been so deeply embedded that she would forever grieve for her Master.

She watched her friend as she sipped her tea. Would she ever be able to take Mark's collar off and find love and commitment with a new Master? Maggie knew she had it in her, the capacity to love and care for someone, but did she have the strength to let the past be the past and move on? If anyone could bring the old LuLu back to them at all it could be Jack, but did he have the equal strength to move on himself? She and Harry both thought their friends could, it would be each helping the other, but it was never going to be easy.

Tea finished, Maggie got up to leave. She hugged her friend and left to get the robe for the ceremony. LuLu stayed in the chair looking at the girl in the portrait over the mantel. They didn't even look like each other anymore. Where had her, what was it Mark used to call it, her "spark for living," where had it gone? Maybe they were right, maybe it was time to either get back in the fight or hang up her spurs.

Her thoughts were interrupted by the knock on the bedroom door. Maggie came in with a box and put it on the sofa. When she opened it, the beautiful, iridescent green fabric that nestled in the tissue papers reminded LuLu of flowing waters. The fabric of the robe would cover her body, but would not leave her any privacy. It was as see-through as any of the robes Mark had had her wear and it was good that her modesty had been left by the wayside long ago.

LuLu took it from Maggie and held it up to her. They looked at the length and figured that, with heels, it would be about right. One of the benefits of the Social Club was the no photography policy. Any pictures members wanted of an event had to be taken either before the guests arrived or after they left so no photos could ever be used against someone. But, for renewals, collarings, or even the formal joining of a couple or family, arrangements could be made for the members of a party to be photographed without anyone else in the shots. For Harry and Maggie's renewal, photos would be taken before the other guests arrived or in the foyer after the ceremony was finished.

LuLu laid the robe over the back of her chair and thanked Maggie. "It really is lovely, where did you get such an interesting fabric? And who made it for you?"

Maggie giggled, "You won't believe! There is a place in Croydon, a shopping mall, where there is a shop that makes wedding dresses and fancy stuff for the gypsy population. A friend of mine was in there and happened to see these fabrics, yours, and mine. I went there a few weeks ago, bought the yard goods, and then had them make the things to my description of what I wanted. The lady thought they would be used as wedding night robes, she had no idea what the real use would be." Maggie was still happy with herself and how clever she had been.

"Well, this one looks grand and I am sure yours will be even better." LuLu stood up, "oh, I think it's about time to dress for dinner and I want a shower before I do." Maggie took the empty box with her and with a hug from LuLu, left to get her own shower and dress for the evening meal.

A half hour later, the two women entered the living room to find the men enjoying a before dinner drink. Martin came in and made drinks for the ladies and within another fifteen had called dinner. Harry took his slave in to eat and Jack offered his arm to LuLu. For a split second she hesitated, but then accepted his arm.

CHAPTER 5

Libby was an excellent cook and the girls left the men to finish their wine. Both Maggie and LuLu took the opportunity to powder their noses and by the time they got back to the living room, the men were just coming in. Jack looked so cool and suave in his white dinner jacket and Harry, poor Harry, no matter how hard he tried, always looked like a rumpled bed. His slave loved the way Harry looked, she picked out all of his clothes for him so she must have loved him that way.

Martin came in with the coffee service and poured each one a brandy. He took his leave and unless LuLu called, he would not be back for the rest of the evening.

At any other time, a quite dinner with friends would be followed by conversation in the living room; perhaps play in the dungeon Mark had built on the top floor, or both. LuLu really didn't have people she was close with that were not lifestylers.

Maggie and Harry had used the dungeon here before and if Mark had been alive, it would have been the most normal thing for her to offer to open it now, but with Jack there, she just didn't know. Would he think he had to play also?

Harry usually plowed right into things without thinking and when Martin left the room he looked at LuLu and asked her about the "playroom." "Jack has never seen it and I know Maggie and I would like to play a bit, it's been a couple of days since we were in the London house…" He finally caught the look his slave was giving him.

He then directed his attention to Jack, "Mark was a real handy one with furniture making. He made quite a few of the pieces at the Social

Club and if I am not mistaken, all of the furniture for your room here," he turned toward LuLu, "right?"

LuLu nodded to him, but Maggie jumped in, "I am sure we all must be tired, it has been a long day and tomorrow night is our renewal ceremony at the Social Club, ..." Now it was her turn to be a bit uncomfortable.

LuLu broke the tension, "I would be happy to open the dungeon. In fact the last time it was used was when you were here on a previous visit." She put her coffee cup on the cart with the rest of the service. "I will go get the key and meet you at the door."

LuLu got up and left. If they wanted to use the room, it was fine with her, she might stay for a few minutes, but Jack could keep them company this time.

Back in their own room, Maggie and Harry were preparing to use the dungeon. "Harry, why did you think it was necessary to ask her that? I don't know if she is ready for that yet and I don't want it to look like we are pushing Jack on her or her on Jack."

"You know they both would go well together," she continued, "but they have to find that out without us. Well, alright, we can give them a little nudge here and there, but playing? I just don't see it."

By the time she was done talking she had changed her clothes and Harry had slipped out of his dinner clothes and was wearing a pair of jeans and a loose fitting shirt. Harry looked at his beautiful slave/wife and still couldn't believe he was the owner of such a wonderful lady. He was so lucky and if she thought he would pass up a chance to play with her, well, that day was never going to come!

Harry knocked on Jack's door as they passed and he came out wearing jeans and a long-sleeved shirt similar to Harry's. Standing at the door of the elevator was LuLu in one of the caftans Maggie had brought her on their last trip from London.

Without a word, LuLu opened the door to the elevator and they all got in for the ride up one flight of stairs to the dungeon. Because of the "coastal muck" the house and all of this part of Texas sat on, basements were either out of the question or would have been so expensive to engineer, most people put their game or playrooms on upper floors.

Mark had put this one in the central part of the attic, accessible only by the elevator.

LuLu put the key in the lock in the elevator control panel and the door slid open. The entryway to the dungeon was marked by a wrought-iron gate with a stylized dragon symbol serving as a latch; the same as Mark's brand. LuLu reached out her hand and caressed the beautifully wrought dragon, lifted it, and let the gate swing open.

A hidden button turned the lights on as soon as the gates released the pressure on it, much like the one that turns on the lights when a closet door is opened. The room was softly lit and the walls were painted a very deep purple.

Mark and LuLu had debated the color choice until one night, on a clear evening; they were on the patio as the sun was going down. The blue of the sky continued to get deeper and deeper until, it reached a point where it turned a beautiful, almost liquid purple. The last rays of red sun mixed with the deep blue lent the sky that color for a few minutes only and Mark knew it was the right color for their dungeon. The next evening he grabbed a camera and took dozens of pictures hoping he caught just the right one to show the color he wanted.

The furniture in the room was, as Harry had mentioned, all made by Mark. The room smelled of leather, wood polish, and still had a hint of the essential oil Mark had always worn. For LuLu, it was a lot of memories to process. She stood aside while the others walked in.

Inside the room, Harry found the dimmer switch that would bring the ambient lights up. He walked to the center of the room and put his toy bag down. Flying from place to place by private plane, made taking his toys with him so much easier since he didn't have to explain to someone who didn't need to know his business what the whips, canes, floggers, wheels, restraints, ropes, etc. were all about and why he wanted to fly with them.

Harry had been in this room a few times, but each time, he admired the way it had been setup. Most dungeons had the St. Andrews cross on a wall, sofas around so people could watch at each appliance's or piece's use, but in this room, it was all Mark. His favorite piece had been the cross and it sat at the center of the room. It was actually a double cross because one slave could be restrained to each side of it and two Masters could use it at the same time or one Master could use two slaves at a time.

Tonight, he wanted his slave on the cross and had been thinking about it all day. He never had been one to trudge from store to store, but with Maggie it was always an adventure. Really, he thought she used those excursions to get him warmed-up for an evening of play.

Today she took him to sit in the Victoria's Secret store and showed him the things she was trying on. The vision of her creamy skin, generous breasts, and shaved pubic mound was always a turn-on for him and with each bra and panty set she tried, he got hungrier and hungrier for her. He loved to watch her spend his money, that is what it was for anyway, and tonight he wanted her, needed to play with her.

Maggie stepped up to the cross and slipped out of the silk robe she wore. She put it over the table near the cross and LuLu brought a small blanket, a couple of towels, and some bottled water from the small fridge. Jack was sitting on the leather sofa with the best view and LuLu hesitated before sitting down.

As she sat down, Jack moved to the end furthest from her. He wanted to sit next to her, but knew it was too soon and anyway, was he ready for this himself? Leave it to Harry to stumble them into this, he only hoped it would all end well for them.

Maggie had locked the cuffs Harry carried in his toy bag onto her wrists and ankles and then he secured her to the arms of the cross. When her hands and feet were securely fastened, he took a padded blindfold from his bag and put it on her. Now her body was totally in his hands. He would use her, her creamy flesh would show the marks of his whip, but he knew her and how far she could be pushed. Tonight was not the time to take her any further that the norm, that was for the next night when the renewal would take place and he would again put his brand on her.

His hand ran down her back and he could feel her push against him. He knew she would take no time at all to bring along to her happy place, but he didn't want it to go too fast. When his hand reached the end of her spine he caressed the faded brand he had put there five years-ago. It was hardly visible, but he knew where he had put it and for him, he knew every inch of his slave's body and knew the new brand would go over the old one nicely.

Cold branding was something he had never heard of until Master Daniel's group took it up as part of their renewal ceremonies. Each Master was the lord of his own house, the owner of all his property, and made all the decisions that affected his property, but the group has certain protocols and rituals they followed and he was agreeable to them. He had known Masters that branded their slaves, he had even attended a collaring where the slave was branded, but he could never do it to his girl. He could not see burning the skin of his slave that way, but the cold brand, although not permanent, was the best way for him and he liked that the group wanted it used and not the branding irons that others preferred.

The cold brands were specially designed and precisely laser cut with each man's symbol. Harry's was the fox. Master Daniel had said Harry reminded him of a fox and it had stuck. The stainless steel brands were placed in a solution of alcohol, water, and dry ice that had been made into a very cold slush. Very special, heavy gloves were worn to guard against being burned by the solution and a tongs was used to put the branding blocks into the solution and take them out when they had reached the desired temperatures. The slave, restrained by cuffs and chains, was then marked with her Master's brand.

It was normal for the slave to scream and for some Master's they used a ball-gag to muffle the sound, but others wanted to hear their slave's cries. Harry used a ball-gag with his, it was upsetting for him to see her cry or hear her scream. Within a short time the cold-burn would form a scab that would stay on the skin for up to two weeks. When it came off on its own, the brand could then be clearly seen. The redness took about a month to disappear, but the brand would last for at least five years, until the next renewal ceremony. It all depended how long the brand was left in contact with the skin about how long it would last, and with Maggie, it was in the nine to twelve second range.

He was ready to start and Maggie had been given enough time to let the anticipation build. Tonight he wanted to start her off with his finger floggers. The two corded floggers fit on the index fingers of each hand and he started to twirl them in opposite directions. The music he had selected had started to play in the background and the sound the cords made as they cut the air was muffled by the beat of the native drums. He looked over at the sofa where Jack and LuLu were sitting and gave a slight nod to let them know he was starting.

When a couple played or sessioned with each other, the people watching would not interfere with them in any way. The spectators usually did not talk or make sudden noises, move around unnecessarily, or distract what was going on. If something they were seeing was upsetting to them, they either waited until it was over or would slip out quietly so as not to disturb what was going on with the players. It was common dungeon etiquette wherever people in the lifestyle played.

Harry played the finger floggers up and down her back and his movements kept pace with the music. When he started focusing on her ass-cheeks, the floggers would strike the top of her ass on the downbeat and the bottom of her ass on the upbeat. The falls of the flogger were fine enough to make contact with her inner thighs on the upbeat and she was beginning to push into the strikes.

After several minutes he put the floggers down and picked up a fine rattan cane he had been wanting to use. It was new and he had never had it used on her so it would be a first for her. He caressed her skin and marveled at the fine lines of welts the finger-floggers had left. He leaned into her and let her feel his weight and he whispered in her ear. "Oh my love, my good girl, tonight we have a new toy. Let me take you to your special place, your dreamy place, mmm, give your body to me and let me make you fly my slave, my beautiful, beautiful slave, mmm…"

She was almost gone, he could read her body so well. He started with some small taps on her back and ass-cheeks then used the cane to rub her, caresses her, he used the tip to caress he inner thighs, her pubic area, and finally he parted her lips and the labia rings she wore made a soft tinkling sound as the tip of the cane brushed against them. The rhythm of the music was beginning to move the cane in his hand and he brought the cane down softly on her back and buttocks.

He began to apply more force as the music got stronger, the beat of the drum fueled the heavier use of his hand. His girl was still pushing into the cane as one song blended into another, and, after several more songs, she finally slipped into sub-space and was flying. How he loved his girl!

Jack watched the play in front of him, but also kept a close eye on LuLu. Like him, this was a scene she had witnessed dozens of times, but he always found the play of others to be highly erotic. He wondered if it would affect LuLu in the same way or if that was something else he would have to work on. Throughout the play Harry did with the finger-floggers, he could see no change in the stony visage LuLu adopted, but as he used the cane, she showed a few signs of emotion.

Both Jack and LuLu saw the signs that Maggie had slipped into her happy place. Her head started to roll to one side and she began to slump against the restraints. Harry continued to use the cane on her as the music pushed him harder and faster, but his slave was oblivious to it all. As the music began to ease up, so did Harry until, near the end, he had replaced the cane with his hands and he was caressing Maggie and rubbing her welts and rising bruises.

Harry let her feel his body next to her and he was again whispering in her ear. He told her over and over what a good girl she was and how much he loved her. He knew how difficult it must have been for her to reach her happy place, but her focus on him and what they were doing together had made it possible for her to fly. After almost twenty-five years together, he knew what it took for her to make the trip and even with all that was going on around them, he was still surprised she had made it happen. At the moment, she was still gone but was slowly coming back. He put the blanket round her shoulders and released her hands and feet from the cross. She slumped against him and he laid her down on the sofa next to the one Jack and LuLu sat on. He held her and rocked her like a baby. For Harry, there was no one else in the world but his slave and he held her close as she continued to emerge from her happy place.

Jack saw LuLu shift in her seat. He recognized the movement and understood what it meant. The scene had affected LuLu, it had turned her on, aroused her, and if Mark was here, she would have been in his arms. But, Mark was not here, he was. Could he, should he reach out to her? Would she rebuff him, run from him, reject him? or, maybe if he put his hand where she could reach it, would she seek out the touch of another person or was she beyond that.

Tentatively, he moved his hand within reach of LuLu. He had crossed the space between them with his hand on the cushion. He didn't look at her, he just left his hand there, it she wanted to, all she had to do was touch his hand. Jack waited, he watched as Maggie finally started to emerge from sub-space and Harry gave her a sip from one of the water bottles. Out of his eye, LuLu had not changed her position, her hands were still in her lap.

Jack was about to pull his hand back when he felt the soft caress of LuLu's hand as it brushed against his. He looked over at her and saw a tear roll down her cheek. She started to pull her hand away, but he held his out to her and after a slight hesitation, she took it. He smiled at her and she lowered her eyes and smiled back. Perhaps she wasn't too far gone after all.

LuLu stood up and went to help Maggie put her robe on. Harry packed his toys back into their carry bag and then took his slave. They all walked to the iron gates and LuLu turned out the lights, closed the dragon symbol that secured the gates, and they descended to the second floor in the elevator. No body spoke. Nothing needed to be said. For each of them, the night was over, or for Harry and his slave, it might be just beginning.

CHAPTER 6

The house had quieted after all of the visitors from the day before. The Chairman had left just after lunch and the play session in the dungeon left Maggie still in bed, sleeping. It was only Harry, Jack, and LuLu for breakfast, but even that was uneventful.

Harry wanted to get back to the room so he could be with his girl, Jack had some phoning to do to check with his contacts about the possible threat from ISIS on LuLu, and LuLu had some work to do to prepare for the move to the beach house. Breakfast was hurried and each went their separate ways. Lunch should bring them all together again.

By lunch LuLu had most of her work finished, Jack had gone to the airport to pick up a package, and Harry and Maggie were ready to eat. She looked wonderful and the soft caresses and winks she and Harry exchanged were almost too private to witness. It did make the loneliness LuLu was feeling that much more pronounced. After lunch, she went to her room to prepare for the night to come.

In her younger days, LuLu could have worked all day, spent all night in the dungeon, and still fulfilled Mark's needs when they got home. Now, however, she needed a good nap before trying to stay up too late. Her bedtime had been set by Mark years ago and he liked to be in bed by eleven. It had stuck with her even after he was gone.

She still slept naked and put his cuff around her ankle, locked it in place, and attached it to the restraint at the end of the bed. This is what made her feel safe. It was how he had trained her and it was as much a part of her nightly ritual as brushing her teeth. The other parts of the "going to bed" ritual were no longer performed and she still missed them.

The first time they slept together Mark had told her how he wanted her to prepare for bed. He had likes, dislikes, and instructions for everything. At first, he made her write everything down, then transcribe it into her word-processor, print it out, and put into her book of rituals, protocols, and rules. After the first few months, she no longer needed to refer to them, it was habit, and the way he wanted his life lived by him and his slave was the way she lived now.

Only after several months did he think she was trained well enough to claim her as his property. During that time there were the long discussions over the contract that spelled out, in detail, the responsibilities of each to the relationship and to the other. It was then that the bond was formally proclaimed at the collaring ceremony when she gave herself to him and he accepted ownership of her.

Many people think that BDSM or their particular niche of it, the Master/slave dynamic is all floggings, restraints, and sex, but it really wasn't. For Mark and her it was the way they lived, day to day. She did know couples that it was only a bedroom or event thing, but theirs was a Total Power Exchange (TPE) 24/7 365 way to live. It had been successful for them for all the years they had known each other.

Every couple was different and one Master might not do the same thing with every slave he has ever owned, it depended on the people. Mark knew how he wanted to live, what things were foundational to him, it was LuLu who had fit into his life, not him fitting into her life.

For most of the "vanilla" couples she knew the biggest problem and source of argument was about who was going to make what decisions; either they both wanted to, neither did, or the one made a decision the other didn't like or accept. In her relationship with Mark, that question of who would make the decisions had been settled from the beginning; Mark would make the decisions. LuLu agreed to give him the power to make them and never regretted it. Even when he lay in a coma, she still did, as Mark would have wanted.

This was the agreement they had between them. The contract they signed spelled out what his responsibilities were to her and her to him, it said what he would do, and what she would in the relationship and they each had limits, "hard limits" that would not be crossed. There was a way to break the contract if it ever came to that, but it was never something she would have done. Each of the contracts they had ever signed together were penned in their own blood. It was not binding in any court of law, but each took an oath to uphold what was in it and that, for them, was more sacrosanct. When she lost Mark, a big part of her died with him.

Tonight, Maggie and Harry would renew their contract and the symbolism and solemnity of the occasion weighed even heavier on LuLu. For now, though, she needed to get herself prepared for the evening's festivities.

The ceremony would not take place until very late in the evening and first they must sit through a dinner at the house Master Daniel had left to the Social Club. The caretakers had seen to its cleaning and upkeep and three of the couples who belonged to the Social Club sat on the board that oversaw its running. She had sat on that board for a couple of years, but didn't attend many of the functions since the accident so excused herself from that responsibility.

The house Master Daniel had left was also used by out of town members when they wanted a friendly place to stay while in town for business or pleasure. Currently, two couples had come to attend the renewal ceremony and were staying in the house. Everything was very convenient, something Master Daniel had insisted upon when he was still alive. Mark and LuLu had stayed with him a couple of times in the house when Mark was posted overseas. LuLu knew the house and grounds very well.

The dungeon was separated from the house itself by a covered walkway. From the outside it looked like any other detached garage, but that would not explain what the other detached garage, the real one, was doing on the opposite side of the house. The area between the dungeon and caretaker's house was for parking and that evening would be filled. The whole area sat in the middle of several acres. A high fence rimmed the property and there was a screen of trees that blocked out any view from three sides. The whole compound was designed for privacy and an electric gate with limited access helped also.

Harry and Maggie had gone to the Club earlier to make sure all of the preparations had been made as they had asked. She had taken the robes she and LuLu would wear and put them in the changing room which was part of the outer area of the dungeon. Harry checked the food that had been sent in by the caterers, the flowers, the wine, and the other things he had ordered had arrived and were ready for the evening's festivities.

The men of the Club, the Masters, had been in contact several times during the last couple of months and knew exactly what Harry wanted for his ceremony. Each man was his own Master, but for collarings, contract ceremonies, or a joining, the Master that was the center of the ceremony could ask his fellow Masters for help and they would give it, much like a Master for a day would be. They knew when it was their ceremony, the other Masters would do the same.

This night would be very formal. The men would all be in their best dress leathers or if they were not part of a leather house or didn't follow leather traditions, in formal attire. The women, slaves of the Masters, would wear the transparent black robes usually worn on these occasions. Tonight, Maggie would be in a creamy beige and LuLu in the emerald green. Lighting, whether or not the fire was lit, music, everything had been planned for and arranged in advance.

Martin drove the car with LuLu and Maggie in it and the men, Harry and Jack followed in another car. Martin would go home and the two couples would use the other car to return later in the night. Although Martin and his wife Libby were aware of LuLu's lifestyle, she never tried to involve them.

Both ladies wore their hair up and although Maggie often wore makeup, LuLu rarely did making it strange she would have as much makeup on as she did. The gowns they wore would be exchanged for the robes before the ceremony, but for now, they as well as the other ladies at the club, were all formally attired.

The caretaker acted as doorman and his wife helped the caterers in the kitchen. Once inside the house, the couples would split up, the men going into the living room to sit with the other Masters and the women to visit with their fellow slaves. Before dinner was announced, the two groups would assemble, the men sitting in a semi-circle in front of the cold fireplace and the women standing behind and to the right of the chairs.

Above the fireplace was the portrait of Master Daniel and his slave/wife Clarisse. As was custom, the evening always started with a toast to the founder. Each year, on the anniversary of Master Daniel's birthday, the group would also gather before the portrait to celebrate.

Dinner was then served and the caterers did the service. The dining room was large enough to seat everyone at one long table, but for this dinner, Harry had wanted the group split into a small head table for the two couples, Harry and Maggie and their seconds, Jack and LuLu, and the rest of the group at the long table. LuLu sat next to Maggie and Jack was on the other side with Harry.

Following a very good dinner, the caterers were given time to clean up and leave. The front gate was then locked and only members were left on the property. The caretaker and his wife were then given time to retire to their cottage. The women usually went to the dungeon first so they could change. The Masters came in as they finished cigars or conversations in the house.

The dungeon had a generous foyer through the double doors at the front. On the left was a changing room for the women and on the right was a locker room where cellphones, valuables, toy bags, or other items could be stored. The women had all changed and the room was almost empty when Maggie and LuLu came in to prepare for the big night.

Maggie really was stunning in the robe she had had made. It was the same kind of material as LuLu's but in a creamy, beige that almost disappeared on her skin. Her red hair was done up in a matching ribbon and showed off the beautiful collar she always wore. The eye shadow she used brought the green of her eyes out and made them even more emerald. She was, at fifty-eight, a stunning woman.

LuLu helped Maggie tie the ribbon that held her robe together and then helped her with hers. She liked the green, a color she never would have chosen for herself, but leave it to Maggie to find just the right shade for her. LuLu didn't wear as much makeup as Maggie, but the light eye shadow and dark red lipstick showed her creamy skin off very well.

One of the other slave girls came to tell them they were about to start the ceremony and wanted to know if they were ready. The friends looked at each other and nodded. Better to get started before nerves set in.

In the main room, the furniture had been moved around so the center of the room was clear. The ceremony would be conducted under the one penlight that shown down from the ceiling. One of the Masters was tasked with turning the lights up, down, or off as the case may be during the ceremony.

The Masters all stood around in a circle, this brotherhood of men, to be witnesses to the proceedings. In the center of the circle, Master Harry stood with Master Jack.

A soft, ambient music played in the background, the lights had all been dimmed, and the Masters stood waiting for the beginning. A line of slave girls, all dressed in sheer black robes, entered from the main doorway, each with an electric candle. Master Daniel was always worried about safety and except for wax play, lighted candles were not used in the dungeon. The slaves took their places before their Masters and each knelt on a cushion at their Master's feet.

Master Jack then stepped forward and opened a leather binder with the program in it. In a strong voice, he asked Master Harry what he was seeking from this company of men, the Masters of the Social Club. Master Harry stepped forward and asked them to witness his renewal ceremony with his slave, Margaret. Each of the Masters nodded their agreement in turn and two of the slave girls stood to accept the order to bring in the slave girl known as Margaret.

The two slave girls left to lead Maggie and LuLu into the circle. The slave girls then rejoined the other slaves in front of their Masters. Margaret and LuLu knelt next to each other in the center of the room. Master Jack then asked slave Margaret if she, of her own free will, wanted to renew her contract with her Master.

Margaret answered in the affirmative. Master Jack then asked slave Margaret to stand before the assembled company of Masters to hear her contract read aloud. LuLu helped Margaret stand and then knelt off to the side while LuLu stood before Master Harry and the room full of people.

Master Jack read the contract. After each section he stopped and asked slave Margaret if she agreed to what was written and each time slave Margaret said a clear, "Yes." When the contract had been read, one of the Masters put a small table in the middle of the couple and the contract was put on it. Another Master brought a tray that held a small bowl, a sharp knife, some sterile swabs, and a fine linen bandage. LuLu held the small bowl while Master Jack used the sterile swab to clean a finger on Master Harry and slave Margaret's hands. He then used the sharp knife to knick each finger and let the blood drip into the small bowl LuLu held. When he finished, he put their fingers together and tied them with the linen bandage.

Holding their bandaged fingers in his hand, Master Jack said, "The blending of their blood strengthens their bond and makes each stronger because of it. Master Harry, slave Margaret, do you both wish to sign this contract of your own free will?" Both said yes and Jack removed the bandage and LuLu used the swabs to clean the wounds and place individual bandages on them.

The small bowl was placed on the table next to the contract. Master Jack took a bottle of red ink and poured a small amount in with the blood. With a tiny spoon he stirred it and sat it next to the contract. Again Jack said, "Slave Margaret, I ask you again, do you wish to sign this contract of your own free will?" When she said yes, he told her to pick up the pen and sign her name.

The only sound in the room was the scratch of the quill pen. When she had finished, she laid the pen down and Master Jack turned to Master Harry. Jack said, "Master Harry, do you accept this slave and if so, sign the contract where indicated." Master Harry picked up the quill and put his name in the line above his slave's. This part of the ceremony was now done, but there was more to it.

The Masters and slaves all gave the couple a round of applause and one of the Masters took the small table from the middle of the group, another put the leather folder with the signed contract on a special cushion and one of the slave girls took the tray with the blood implements and put it out of the way.

The slaves all turned their candles up to the brightest setting while the small table was brought back, this time with the liquid slush that would cool the branding block. LuLu helped Maggie remove her robe and she stood before the group naked except for her shoes. Two of the Masters helped Harry secure Maggie to the chain suspended from the ceiling. Her hands were cuffed and attached above her head and her ankles were secured to eyebolts in the floor.

Maggie was now secure with her back to the group. Jack and Harry had donned heavy rubber gloves and Harry had the tongs that he would use to remove the brand from the slush. LuLu used a sterile swab to clean the area on Maggie's back where Harry would put the brand. After she used the swab, LuLu took the ball-gag from the table and put it in Maggie's mouth and secured it behind her head. She then put the blindfold on her.

The stainless steel block had been in the cold slush for a long enough time and in a swift movement, Jack helped Harry take it from the slush with the tongs, turn it so it was right side up, and Harry put the cold metal onto Maggie's skin in the exact place he wanted it. Jack counted out loud the seconds the brand was left on her skin.

Maggie felt the cold hit her back and screamed into the ball-gag. She tried not to pull away, but her body's defenses were stronger than she was and she started to twist. The restraints kept her from moving and by the time Master Jack finished his count, the brand was removed and LuLu was spraying the area with an aerosol that would help kill the pain. Within minutes, she was taken down and the pain was bearable. The smile on her face was brighter than the light in the room.

The restraints were taken off and the same two Masters removed the table and other equipment once again. In its place, they put a larger table and chair that Mark had made for the dungeon when it was first built. It allowed the slave to be restrained with cuffs on each front leg of the chair but the seat was split so the slave's pubic area would be totally exposed. The arms could be secured to the arms of the chair but tonight, Maggie had her arms free and only her ankles were fastened into the attached cuffs. The chair was placed on the table.

Jack came forward with a small bag and handed it to Harry. Inside the bag was a gold ring and LuLu handed him the small pliers. The ring was open and Harry put the new ring through one of the rings that pierced her labia. It joined the others that were there. Harry then closed the ring with the pliers and handed them back to LuLu.

LuLu helped Jack remove the restraints from Maggie's ankles, the chair was put back on the stage, and then she helped her put her robe back on. The last thing she did was remove the blindfold and tie the ribbon on her robe to close it. The ceremony was over. The lights came up in the room and the slaves all turned off their candles. The Masters and slaves all applauded and it seemed like everyone started talking at once.

Jack looked at LuLu. The green fabric of her robe was so transparent it left nothing to the imagination. He liked what he saw and realized for the second time he felt he wanted her. She was busy putting the things away from the ceremony and he reached out to help her. Their hands touched and for an instant, he felt a slight shock.

LuLu looked up at Jack. She had noticed it on the drive over, how handsome he was in his dress leathers. As casual as he could be at other times, for this occasion he was resplendent in a finely made jacket, pants, vest, and tie of black leather. Many men liked the heavy bull hide, but his was soft and pliable like doeskin. His boots, however, were heavy jackboots that had softened from years of care and use. His late wife must have put hours into getting them that soft.

Mark had trained LuLu to be comfortable wearing little or nothing while in the club or during private dinner parties at their home when entertaining lifestyle friends. It didn't bother her that Jack or anyone else could see her almost nude body, she was proud of it and did not feel the need to hide behind modesty. She noticed that Jack was looking at her and that he was seemingly pleased with what he saw.

Several of the slaves were overweight and their Masters liked them that way. She had once been heavier than was healthy for her, but when Mark had his accident, she found it hard to eat as much as before and the weight started to melt off her. In the last few years since his death, she had kept up a work schedule that often interfered with her meal schedule. She put the work first and that kept her from putting the weight back. Now, she was in a good place with her weight and the result was a trim body that looked good without clothes.

Harry and Maggie were still on London time and both looked like they needed rest. Jack asked if they were about ready to leave and Maggie asked if they could go to the foyer and get their pictures taken to mark the celebration. Harry agreed and the four of them went the foyer, the doors to the dungeon were closed, and a camera was set up to take their pictures. Once the camera was secured, the doors were opened again. Master Daniel's wishes about 'no cameras' was still in force.

The Contract was placed in the dungeon vault along with the contracts of the other members. The brand was put in the glass case that held the others belonging to members and everything was locked away until the next time they were needed.

LuLu looked at the brand that Mark had used on her that last time. Jack was looking over her shoulder and said, "very nice, it must have looked beautiful on you." LuLu turned to look at him then lowered her eyes and left the room.

The girls used the dressing room to put their gowns back on and the robes they had worn back in the boxes to take home. Boxes in hand, they met the two men waiting for them in the foyer. The men took the boxes from their ladies and they all walked to where the car was parked. The drive back to LuLu's was made in silence.

Martin was there to open the door as they drove up and he took the car around to the garage as they went inside. It was no different than if they had just come in from a night at the theatre or a party. They went into the living room where a coffee service was sitting, waiting for them and the brandy was also on the service cart. The group all decided a brandy was in order and Jack poured each a drink.

Martin came back in and asked if anything else would be needed before he retired for the night. LuLu told him he could go and everyone wished him good night. Harry and Maggie would be leaving the next day and Jack would be staying on to "watch" over her. Harry and Maggie finished their drinks and decided it was time for bed.

Jack was only half way finished with his drink and LuLu stayed with him until he'd finished. Together they ascended the stairs. Jack walked her to the bedroom door and took her hand. She didn't pull away from him and that was good. He raised her hand to his lips and brushed it with a kiss. "Sleep well" was all he said.

CHAPTER 7

Harry and Maggie were due to leave just after lunch. Their last meal with LuLu and Jack was filled with talk about the ceremony they had had the night before and Maggie wanted to know when LuLu would be coming back to London for a visit. "Why don't you come for Christmas this year? It's been ages since you've had a good English Christmas, please come." She loved that particular holiday and always had something planned. "We would love to have you both if you wanted to make it a foursome!"

It seemed Maggie was going to be as pushy about LuLu and Jack as Harry had been, but LuLu wasn't going to commit to anything. "I will let you know later, you know I like to go see the grandchildren then and visit with my son."

"Too bad you can't bring them over; our house hasn't had children for Christmas since I was a child. Think about it." Maggie and Harry never had children and it was only on special holidays that it seemed to make a difference to them.

When she met Mark, she was unsure of getting into a relationship. It took him several months of talking and explaining about his lifestyle, but once he had started with her, she quickly became attached to him and fell very deeply in love. Mark knew she was wary of having children and convinced her their lifestyle would not hinder them. He had known Master/slave couples who led full BDSM lives and they had kept it separate from their children's lives.

After he had collared her, they spent the next two years just enjoying each other. Finally, she knew he was right about the idea of having children. Within two months he had her pregnant with their son.

The child was born while they were living outside of the country and LuLu didn't have relatives near to help her care for him or to interfere in her being a wonderful mother. Mark had always told her he just wanted her to be the best mother she could be to their son. This was Mark's only child and when he was old enough to start middle school; Mark had asked his company to return him to the United States.

For all of the advantages living in a foreign country had as far as leaning and living a language, Mark and LuLu were as American as they came. They both liked NFL football, backyard barbeques, and the Fourth of July. They wanted their son to have the best America had to offer.

Mark found them a house in a good school district and Daniel Fields, head of Mark's company, loved having them back. Mark had been the first Master that he had mentored and felt toward him like a son. Master Daniel and his slave/wife had never had children so Mark and LuLu were treated like family. Master Daniel doted on their son like any proud grandfather would.

When their son left for college, Mark started building the house where she now lived. In all the years their boy was growing up, they had never let him know about their "lifestyle" and to this day, he still did not know. LuLu's son lived on the other side of the country and only visited on special occasions. His marriage a few years before cut down on the frequency of his visits even more. They talked on the phone each week and they had a close relationship, but his work kept him far away. LuLu knew she could get on a plane and see him and her grandchildren whenever she wanted.

LuLu quit thinking about her family long enough to see off her friends. She and Jack stood at the door and wished them a safe journey. When the door closed, LuLu headed back to her office and Jack asked if he could join her. He wanted to talk to her about the trip to New York and her plans to go to the beach house.

Alice, LuLu's secretary, was just about to leave when LuLu and Jack walked into the office. Since Martin had taken Harry and Maggie to the airport, Alice offered to bring the coffee service in before she left. Today she was only there for a half day and the coffee service would be the last thing she would do before leaving. Libby had added a few slices of cherry cake with the coffee.

LuLu sat in her desk chair and Jack sat opposite her. He put a couple of files on the desk between them and after he took a couple sips of his coffee he was ready to get started. As was her habit, LuLu liked to doodle while other people talked.

"I talked to a couple of people I know in the Company (CIA) and they have no other information to give me. I did find out that your pictures were not the only ones on the thumb drive, but of the ones on there, yours were among eight different people the boys at MI5 could not identify. They were able to put names on all but two and Interpol thinks one of them maybe in Hong Kong and the other is still a mystery." Jack looked up from his notes. "Now they are trying to determine what the common link is between the people who were in the photos might be."

Jack went on, "We know what you were doing in London, and where you had been photographed, the other people were also in London or a British city. We still don't see a common thread."

LuLu stopped doodling, "Is there any chance this is just a case of mistaken identity? I mean, why me? Could it really be because I have helped move these people out of the area?"

Jack looked up from his notes. He had wondered that same thing himself, but as Saxby had said when he brought this to their attention, with three pictures it meant someone was out to get her. Now they just had to keep her safe and hopefully figure out the "why" before anyone could try to get to her. It did mean her travel would have to be restricted. In this house, or the beach house they could control who could get close enough to her to harm her, any place else would be an uncontrolled environment and that put them at a disadvantage.

Jack thought, and the Chairman and Saxby agreed, that the key to the "why" could be a "who." Maybe it wasn't so much what she was involved in but who might have been one of the "packages" that had been moved? "LuLu, do you have a list of the people you have moved?"

"Uh, no, Mr. Anthony just lets me know how many people and I contact either someone in Paris or Malta. Mostly they have family that are making arrangements for them from there. Is it important who they were?" Her doodling was over for this conversation, it was too serious to take her mind off what he was saying. "I suppose I could get a list. Oh, damn, Alice is gone. Let me get the emails from Mr. Anthony."

LuLu got up and pulled a thumb drive from her desk drawer. She opened the door to Alice's office and Jack saw her plug it into the laptop sitting on the desk. In a couple of minutes she was back with the drive. Plugging it into her computer, she started scrolling through some emails. A quiet "woosh" was heard in the background. LuLu went back to Alice's office and emerged with a stack of paper from the printer. She closed the office door and sat back down at her desk.

Handing the paper to Jack, LuLu told him. "These are copies of all of the emails I have gotten from Mr. Anthony. It looks like, by my count, it maybe more than a hundred thirty people. Hmm, I guess I lost track of the number, anyway, I can ask him for the roster if you need it."

Jack was paging through the emails, "It is a good place to start. Please do it."

LuLu turned her attention to the email she sent out to Mr. Anthony. 'Need an up-to-date manifest.' Simple but he knew what she wanted. She hit the send button and knew he would probably get it within a few minutes, if he was still up. It was the middle of the night in Cyprus so it might be the next day before it was answered.

Jack put the papers down and opened the next file. "I talked to Alice this morning and she gave me the copy of you reservations for New York. I need to modify them, but I wanted to tell you first."

LuLu nodded for him to go on. "I have a better place for you to stay, it has all of the security features to keep you safe, but first I need to know what you will be doing there. Is this a shopping trip, business, what?"

LuLu frowned at the word "shopping." "Jack, I don't do, 'shopping.' If I can't buy it over the internet or send someone else out to buy it, well, then I probably don't need it. As for the purpose of the trip; I bought a vintage Bentley from my godparents when I was in London a couple of weeks ago. It is arriving in New York and I want to make arrangements with a shop there to receive it, check it's servicing, and then arrange to have it sent on to me."

Jack liked cars, but he was more a vintage muscle-car kind of guy. "Why? You're not going to drive it here, are you?"

LuLu was beginning to get annoyed. "Yes, I plan on driving it. That was the car I drove while I was in college." She saw the puzzled look on his face. Maybe it was time to explain.

"My father was a veteran of WWII. Before the war started for the United States, he and a friend of his went to Canada and joined the Royal Canadian Air Force. At the time they needed pilots for the air war over Britain, the Germans were killing pilots at an alarming rate. One of the men father flew with was Sir George Gordon-Clark. Actually, he wasn't' Sir George until a few months into the war when his father passed away and he inherited the title from him, but that is not the point. Anyway, father and the man I call Uncle George got to be good friends and when he was on leave, they would stay at this place George's father had in the country, Mickleham Hall."

"Uncle George had a sister, Elizabeth, and I think my father might have taken her to a couple of dances, but nothing very serious. She later met a young lord from Scotland, Ian McAlister and fell head-over-heels. They married and she became Lady Elizabeth McAlister. Ian was killed within a year and she remained his widow."

"Anyway, when Pearl Harbor happened, father was sent back to the States and went into the Army Air Corps. There were not many pilots who had flown against the Germans, at least not that many who were still alive. They made him a flight instructor; he had to teach American pilots how to fight the enemy. He hated being on the sidelines, as he put it, and kept asking to go back to fight. Finally, he got his wish and he spent the rest of the war in England. He flew out of one of the English bases and, fortunately for me, lived to see the war's end."

"When I was ready to go to college, it was the late 60's early 70's; father didn't like all of the turmoil on the campuses here. He had kept close contact with Sir George and Lady Elizabeth, I used to call her Aunt "Lilith", and we visited them a couple of times when I was little. They suggested to father that he let me come to university in London and they could look after me. That is how I got to London, to the university there, and how my friendship with Lady Margaret, uh, Maggie, started."

She took a sip of her now cold coffee, made a face, and continued. "By the time I was in university, Uncle George had had to sell Mickleham Hall to pay the inheritance taxes and many of the best pieces of furniture and art work had been put in the London house. Lady Elizabeth was a widow and she lived with George in London. When her Ian died, the title in Scotland passed to a distant cousin of his in Australia, but she will be known as Lady Elizabeth for the rest of her life."

"Uncle George has a heart condition and has had for years. His doctor tried to stop him from driving a long time ago and when I was there in university we had an agreement. I could drive the car to school if I would drive them to the country on weekends. It worked fine and I really fell in love with the car. It has been serviced over the years, but not driven more than a few miles every month to keep it running. When they sold the London house, I finally convinced them it was time to let me buy the car and bring it here. Kind of like letting it go to a good home."

Jack put some more coffee in his cup and motioned to LuLu. She held her cup out, "Please. Anyway, while I was in London I made arrangements to have the car shipped. The garage they have used to do the service has changed hands a couple of times over the years and the last guys, well, they suggested a company in New York to do the inspections, service, and stuff before they would send it on to me. I just need to contact them because the car should be arriving the beginning of this next week. That, Jack, is what I will be doing in New York."

She took the cup of coffee and they both sat in silence. "LuLu, I am trying to help out here, but if you don't want me to, just say the word and I'll get Saxby to send this Millbury guy over."

She looked at him, her tone might have been better, but she always bristled when people just took it for granted that she would waste her time shopping. "Look, I'm sorry, it's just, that, well, I get a little off when people make assumptions about me. Sorry, I want you to stay. Anyway, I think we put Saxby's nose out a bit when the Chairman asked you to stay." She reached across the desk to pat his hand.

"Tell me where you want me to stay in New York." She hoped they could get off the subject of 'hurt feelings' and wanted to change the conversation. "I suppose as long as you think it's the best place, I'll stay there."

Jack squeezed her hand and she didn't pull away. He held onto it and looked her in the eyes, "Don't worry, it will be the perfect place. Great views of Central Park and close to everything." He let her hand go, he didn't want to move too fast and scare her away. "We can leave this afternoon if you like."

LuLu figured he was talking about the Plaza Hotel; she had stayed there quite often over the years and liked it. It would be fine with her. "Alright Jack, this afternoon it is. Will we be in time for dinner in the city or do we want a box lunch for the plane?"

He smiled, "if you want to take a snack for the plane, that's fine, but I think a late supper in New York would not be hard to find."

She stood up and Jack left the office when she did. They both went upstairs, him to the room he had been using and her to the master suite. She still had a couple of things to put in a bag and he had his own packing to do.

CHAPTER 8

The little business jet with the Foundation logo on its tail pulled up to the hanger at Teterboro Airport in New Jersey and was pulled into one of the open hangers. When the jet was inside and the doors to the hanger closed, the steward opened the aircraft's door and put the stairs down.

A black Suburban pulled up and a large man who was obviously a plain-clothes security guard came up to the stairs. He saw Jack and broke into a big grin. "A little different plane than the last time you were in town. Need a lift?"

Jack reached out his hand and the big man pumped it several times. "Just need a ride to town. Any news here?"

The man was about to answer when LuLu started down the stairs. A smile lit up the man's face and he reached out a hand to help the "lady down the stairs, Ma'am?" Jack gave him a playful punch and told him he would take care of the lady. Then he turned back to Jack.

"Jack, we are still trying to find a link, but right now, we would like to see that list." He again turned his attention to LuLu, "Sorry Ma'am, this old SEAL must not have learned any manners, my name is Jeremy and I used to work with him."

LuLu shook Jeremy's hand. "Thank you."

Jack took her elbow and steered her toward the open back door of the car. She got inside and the two men stood outside talking for a few minutes while the luggage was being loaded in the back. They got in and began the ride into the City.

The two men continued their talk as the skyline of the city loomed and then consumed them. LuLu must have dozed for a few minutes because before long, Jack was waking her up.

She looked around and the only thing she saw was parked cars. Instead of letting them out in front of the hotel, Jeremy had driven them to the parking garage. A porter had their luggage on a cart and LuLu just saw him disappear into what must have been the service elevator.

Jack shook Jeremy's hand and thanked him for the ride in. Before he rolled away, Jeremy said goodbye to LuLu and wished her a pleasant evening. Jack took her carryon bag and they got into the open elevator.

It had been sometime since LuLu had stayed at the Plaza, actually, before it had been closed for a couple of years for renovations. She didn't think much of what they had done with the elevators. It was nice, but it didn't have the Plaza logo on the doors like they used to. Maybe this was the residential section of the hotel.

The elevator stopped and before her was a lovely foyer with two doors leading off it. One door had a name on it but the other, was rather plain and only bore a number. The door with the name opened and a large black woman stood in the entry. "Mr. Harris, welcome home."

It took LuLu a few seconds to understand what was happening. She whirled around on Jack, "This isn't the Plaza?!"

Jack laughed, "I never said anything about a hotel and this is much nicer than the Plaza." He took her inside. "Hi Flo, thanks for waiting for me. Did you get the room ready and the supper for us?"

He had directed his questions to the woman at the door. "Yes, the room is ready and the supper is in the icebox." The woman looked at LuLu and then at Jack. She had been his housekeeper since he bought the apartment from her former employer. This was not the kind of woman he usually came here with and he never wanted the extra bedroom made up.

Jack saw her eyeing LuLu. "Flo, this is Louise Denton-Jones. I am helping her company find out who might want to hurt her and she is going to be staying with us for a few days."

Flo's look softened. So, she wasn't one of 'those kind' of women. It was about time Mr. Jack found him a decent woman. He had been alone too long and it was not good for a man to be left alone. Lord knew what kind of trouble they could get into!

Flo turned back to Jack. "I'll be leaving then. Be back at six to get your breakfast." She looked at LuLu, "is there anything special you want for breakfast ma'am?"

LuLu shook her head, "No, whatever he's having is fine with me."

Flo picked up her purse and bag from the hall table and left. Jack and LuLu were alone.

Jack moved past her and told her to follow him. Before she could move, a knock and call of "hello" could be heard coming from another room. Jack pushed open a door on the right and LuLu saw the kitchen. The plain door she had seen in the foyer was open and the man who had taken their bags was standing there asking where Jack wanted them.

The man set them on the kitchen floor, took his cart, and closed the door. Jack took the bag for LuLu and again told her to follow him.

He led her to the door of what would be her room. The drapes had been pulled back and a picture window with the lighted buildings of New York providing the lighting, greeted her. Jack turned the lights to the room on and put her bag on the bed.

He left her there.

She looked around the room and found it to be very large for a New York apartment. Besides the big window, it had a lovely four-poster bed, high ceilings, and a nice little sitting area in front of a modern gas fireplace. A door on the left held a full bath and when she opened the door on the right, a large walk-in closet completed the suite.

LuLu put her briefcase on the little desk in front of the window, her jacket on a hanger in the closet, and turned to find Jack leaning against the doorjamb watching her. She smiled. "I, uh, I'm sorry if I misunderstood. When you described the place we would be staying, I thought, well, my mind just processed, "Plaza Hotel". Sorry."

Jack smiled. "It's ok, I suppose I should have told you, but, well, I don't' really use this place very much and it seemed like a good time to come here."

"I put state of the art security equipment in when I bought it and with me just down the hall; I figured this was the best place for me to keep you safe." He motioned to the window. "Besides, the views are terrific. Now, about supper. Would you be interested in a picnic?"

He saw the surprise in her eyes. "I, uh, guess, but where do you do that in New York at this time of night?"

He laughed, "You just leave that to me. I'll come and get you when I'm ready. Take some time to unpack and change if you want. Supper will be ready in no time."

Jack left and LuLu did want to change. If took her a few minutes to unpack and she put a skirt and blouse on that was more casual than the business suit she had been wearing. Mark had never liked her in pants and she only wore them when riding or flying. Most of the time, though, she wore well-tailored suits or dresses.

Jack knocked on the door and she saw he had changed to jeans and a loose tee shirt. He took her hand and led her down the hall to the kitchen. He asked if she liked white or red wine.

"White if you have it," she said, "but not too cold please." He pulled a bottle from the wine cooler and asked her to follow.

Jack took her to the living room. It was a large room that had the same view of the City as her room. The one wall was made of glass doors and they were open to the terrace beyond. A table and some chairs were set up with plates and food. Jack held a chair for her and poured some of the white wine into her glass.

The view was breathtaking. They were high enough to avoid most of the traffic noise, but she was sure this was not the top floor. Jack must have been a mind reader.

"Actually, it is the penthouse; this is just the first floor. My room and office are on the floor above." He picked up an open beer bottle that sat in front of his plate. "I bought this from the owner's estate just after 9/11. The Feds had asked a lot of us who were in the security field to come and help "connect dots" and try to prevent another attack. I figured it was cheaper to own a place than pay for hotels."

She turned her attention to the food. It was all the kinds of things one would expect to find at a picnic; cold fried chicken, potato salad, beans, coleslaw, fruit, and on the table next to it, a pie. Jack waved at the food. "I like simple things, beer, football, and comfort food."

They spent the next hour enjoying the view, eating, and for the first time, they really had a chance to talk. Jack told her about his wife Emily and then told her some funny stories about himself. For the first time, he actually heard LuLu laugh, a genuine, real laugh.

"You should do that more often." He told her.

She looked puzzled, "Do what?"

"Laugh. That is the first time since I met you that you really laughed. It has a nice sound to it; you should do it more often." He reached over to fill her wine glass. "I know we have been involved in some very serious things, but, you really do need to laugh more."

She took a sip of the wine. She had the feeling it was time to go back inside. A gust of wind made her shudder. Jack saw it and thought she might be chilled. The weather in New York was certainly not as hot as Texas. He took her glass and put it on the table. "Let's go in. I'll put these things in the fridge and be right back."

Jack left her in the living room. He put the plates on the second shelf of the service cart and the remains of the food on top, rolled it into the kitchen, and was back in the living room in minutes. "Flo will take care of the dishes tomorrow."

LuLu look up at him, "Nonsense, I can do dishes. Let me help." Before he could object, she was off the sofa and heading for the kitchen. All he could do was follow.

In the kitchen LuLu had started taking the dirty plates from the cart and was rinsing them in the sink. Jack pulled on one of the lower cabinet doors and the dishwasher appeared. "We can put them in here."

Dishes packed in the washer, the rest of the things would be handled by Flo when she got there in the morning. LuLu was drying her hands when Jack came up to her.

"Come sit with me for a while." He took the towel from her and led her back to the living room. He took a remote control from the fireplace and pushed a button. The glass doors to the terrace slid shut and he put the remote back where he got it. On the coffee table was another remote and with it he dimmed the lights and soft music began playing in the background.

Now LuLu was sure it was time for her to go to bed; this was not how she had imagined the evening and didn't want to deal with having to turn Jack away. She started to walk toward the hall that would take her to her room, but he pulled her back. He put his arm around her waist and bent down to kiss her.

Her cheeks flushed bright red and her hand braced against his chest. "Please, don't. I, uh, I can't."

He took her hand from his chest and holding both at her side, kissed her before she could protest further. He felt her stiffen then begin to weaken. He let one hand go and put the other behind her head and held her to him while the kiss deepened. "Yes, LuLu, you can." Then he let her go.

Several things ran though her mind, but most of it was a jumble. She wanted to hit him, lash out, and hurt him, but mostly, she didn't want him to stop.

He could see the confusion in her eyes. Then he saw the determination she had used as a shield descend upon her and knew she was again thinking like Mark's widow. He started to take her hand again but she backed up and shook her head.

"I, um, I think it's time for me to get some sleep." LuLu turned and left the room.

Jack shook his head, it was his fault, he shouldn't have tried anything like that, at least not yet. He picked up the remote and turned the music off and the light back up. Then he remembered something. He went down the hall to the room where LuLu was staying and knocked on the door.

A few seconds later, she came to the door and opened it. Jack apologized for bothering her. "I forgot to get the name of the company the people in London recommended to you. Can you give it to me?"

LuLu shook her head and walked back into the room. She had been ready to undress for bed when he knocked and now she was glad she hadn't. She took her laptop off the desk and handed it to him. "It's in a file called London trip, number 14. It has all of the info on the shipping, the manifest, and the people who were recommended here." She stepped back, into the room.

Jack retreated into the hall. "Thank you, well, good night. Please sleep well and if you need anything, just pickup that phone and press "1.""

LuLu shut the door. Jack took the computer and went to his own room. He opened it and found the file he wanted. He copied the information and was about to close the machine. Then he saw, in the list of files, a folder called "Rules_Protocols_Rituals". He wanted to see that file.

He put the laptop on his bed and prepared to sleep. He finished in the bathroom and got in his bed and picked up the machine. He brought that file up and started reading.

For the next couple of hours Jack entered the life of Master Mark and slave LuLu. All of the rules Mark had made LuLu write down over the years, the protocols he had for various things she did, and the rituals he had her follow, it was all here. He probably shouldn't have read it, but he wanted to understand her and this was one of the easiest ways to do that.

He read about how Mark wanted his coffee served, his shirts ironed, and that he didn't like broccoli. The ritual they had for bedtime was especially graphic and even a little titillating. Hmm, he wondered if she still did that. And then there were dozens of petty likes and dislikes that all went in to making up how Mark had wanted his life and what LuLu did to make it happen.

He then got to the list of punishments. From minor to major, there was a consequence for every incidence of wrongdoing. For a first time infraction it was five strikes with the cane and the second time of the same rule, ten strikes. Disrespectful attitude or speech, poor use of language, the list went on and on. The lesser of any punishment was having to write out a passage from a book.

He finally turned the machine off, put on his robe, and took it to the living room where LuLu would find it in the morning. He had pried into her life enough for one night.

While Jack was snooping in her life, LuLu was having trouble sleeping. She had taken her clothes off and hung them in the closet, done what she needed in the bathroom, then pulled the rope from her suitcase. It had a loop on one end that fit around the leg of the bed and a clip at the other end. She then took the heavy black leather cuff from the bag and using the small padlock hanging from the clasp, locked it around her ankle. She fastened the clip on the rope to the "O" ring on the cuff. Now, she was ready for bed.

She pulled the sheet up around her naked body and tried to go to sleep. Jack's kiss was bothering her, though. She was sure she hadn't given him any encouragement to do that, but she thought over everything she had done in the last few days to make sure. She tossed and turned and thought, and remembered, but nothing could explain why he would have done that.

Finally, more than two hours after trying to sleep, she got up, undid the restraint holding her cuffed ankle, and went into the bathroom. She looked around for a glass to drink water and didn't find one.

LuLu opened the drawer where she had put one of her caftans and slipped it over her head. As she walked, the lock on the cuff made a light clinking sound. She headed to the kitchen and opened one of the cabinets to find a glass. She filled it with water and turned out the lights. She opened the door to the living room and with the lights from outside streaming into the room; she saw her laptop on the coffee table.

She picked it up and started down the hall. All of the lights in the apartment came on and a high-pitched squeal split the air. A door flew open and Jack, naked as the day he was born, burst into the hall with a gun in his hand. The noise and movement frightened her and she dropped the glass but held her laptop to her chest.

By the time Jack knew what had happened, LuLu was shaking. The water was mixed with the broken glass and when Jack took a step towards her, he heard the crunch as his bare foot found a piece. He shouted and it just made matters worse.

Jack secured the gun and put it on the table. He hopped to the couch and put his bleeding foot on his knee to remove the piece of glass. LuLu realized what had happened and knelt down in front of him to help. She asked him where a first-aid kit was and he told her where to find one. By the time she got back, Jack had taken one of the pillows from the sofa and covered his nakedness.

LuLu again knelt before him and opened the kit. Jack yelped when she cleaned the wound and then again when she put some antibiotic cream on it. The bandage came next and he was patched up. She put the kit back where she found it and found a broom closet and started picking up the glass and clearing up the water. Jack watched her as she worked.

He liked the way she took charge and did what needed to be done, without being told. She didn't panic, but went right to work. Now she turned her attention back to Jack. "What, was all that about? You nearly scared me to death!"

Jack laughed, "I told you this place had a great security system. Since I thought you were in bed, I set the system and it worked just like it is supposed to. It didn't know you would be up wandering around."

LuLu thought about it then had to laugh also. "You did look pretty funny bursting into the hall wearing only a gun!"

Jack blushed and it made LuLu wonder if she had said the wrong thing. "Madam, I will have you know that is one of the finest handguns on the market. No undressed security professional would ever want to be without one." They both laughed.

Jack looked down at the cuff on LuLu's ankle. "I take it you were in bed and just needed some water. I thought you would've been asleep hours ago."

LuLu blushed. "Maybe it is the strange bed, but yes, I did come looking for water. Then I saw my laptop and picked it up on my way back to the room. That is when all this happened. Now, I guess it is time for me to get back to bed. Goodnight Jack."

She turned to leave. Jack stood up and put the pillow back on the sofa. He reached out his hand to her. Don't go, I still need to turn out the lights and set the alarm. Wait until I do that."

She turned back, saw he was again uncovered, and just stood there. "Could you, uh, please put something on?"

He chuckled. "Ok, but don't go until I get back." He left the room and got a bathrobe from one of the rooms down the hall. He turned out lights as he went until only the ones in the kitchen and living room were still burning. He doused the kitchen lights, set the alarm, and came back to where LuLu was standing.

He pulled the robe around himself and asked her, "Is this better?" LuLu nodded. Jack took her arm and walked her back down the hallway. She opened the door to the bedroom. He pointed to the cuff on her ankle. "Show me" was all he said.

LuLu looked at him and thought she understood what he wanted. She went to the bed, sat down, and attached the restraint to the cuff.

"No" he said, "I want to tuck you in." He waited for her to let that sink in. She nodded and stood up, removed the caftan and stood before him naked. She sat back down on the bed and got under the sheet. He sat next to her and tucked the covers around her body, then leaned down and kissed her goodnight. "Do you think you can stay in bed now?" She nodded to him. "Good, then stay here until it's time for breakfast."

Jack turned off the light and left the room. Sleep for LuLu was now impossible.

The sun had been up for over an hour before LuLu undid her restraint, unlocked the cuff, and dressed for breakfast. She got to the kitchen to find Flo taking dishes from the washer. Flo turned and told her that she would have her breakfast ready in no time.

She showed LuLu to the dining room and there was another stunning view of New York. Flo told her that "Mr. Harris had his breakfast early and said he would be back in time for lunch."

LuLu ate by herself and then went to her room to retrieve her laptop. She had come to New York for a reason and it was time to get to work. She copied the name and address of the shipping company and the service company into her PDA then dialed the phone numbers for each place. The shipping company was closed, it was, after all a Saturday, but the service company answered.

A man with a slight accent answered the phone. She told him what she was wanting and gave him the name of the person who had told her about him. He immediately warmed up to her and told her that, yes, they could do the work on the Bentley. She asked what their hours were and exactly where they were located. He told he would be there until two and how to find the shop.

LuLu wrote a note to Jack and told him where she would be. On her way out of the apartment, she asked Flo what the address was of the apartment and she wrote it down on her note pad. Flo told her she might like to wait for Mr. Harris to come back, but LuLu wanted to get this out of the way.

On the ground floor of the building a doorman hailed her a taxi. She hadn't been gone more than two minutes when Jack got out of a plain black car. He leaned in and said something to the driver. The doorman tipped his hat and Jack told him good morning.

As soon as he opened the door to his apartment, Flo was at the door. Jack asked for LuLu and when Flo said she had left he became angry. "Where did she go? Did you try to stop her?"

Now Flo was worried. Mr. Harris was one of the most easygoing people she had ever met and for him to be all worked up like this got her upset. "No sir, she just said she had some work to do, wrote you this note, and left."

Jack took the elevator down and questioned the doorman. He told Jack that, yes, he just called a taxi for the lady, but no, he didn't hear what address she had given him. Jack pulled out his cell phone and started making calls.

In a few minutes a black car like the one that had let him off came screeching up to the door and Jack got in before it could pull back into the busy morning traffic.

The shipping company was closed and that left the service company. He had the address and he gave it to the driver of the black car. They were now at least fifteen minutes behind her and Jack was worried.

A friend of his at MI5 had looked at what LuLu had been doing in London when she was there the last time. She had bought the car just like she said, but the agency that serviced it for Sir George had indeed changed hands many times. The last time it had been bought by a couple of brothers whose parents had emigrated from Syria when they were children. Both brothers had worked fixing some high-end cars and when the shop had become available, they borrowed enough from family members to buy it.

The name of the shop had never changed and anyone phoning would think it was still owned by locals. Jack's friend from MI5 asked someone to take a look at it and what they found was troubling. One of the brothers was a well-adjusted British national with a local wife, three children, and all the trappings of normal life.

The other brother was an angry young man who had fallen under the spell of a man from the local mosque. He had never felt British at all, quite the opposite; he was and would always be an outsider. He was just the kind of man the recruiters from ISIS were looking for, disaffected nationals.

Jack had spent most of this morning looking at the information from MI5 and trying to cross match it with the service company in New York. One of his former employees, the man driving the car, had told him he would look into it. It was a Saturday and no one expected anything to happen before Monday. But then, Jack hadn't counted on LuLu plowing ahead with what she thought she needed to do.

Traffic being what it is in New York, they finally got to the building where the service company was located. Over a large garage-type door was a faded sign, "Foreign Car Service" and some logos of various European cars. An almost indistinguishable Bentley logo was among them. There was no one around but a taxi, with its driver, was parked on the street.

Jack and the driver stopped a ways back to wait. Jack was about to call the NYPD to ask for assistance when LuLu and a short, balding man emerged from the garage door. She shook his hand and he went back into the building. LuLu walked to the taxi and got in.

The driver of the black car followed the taxi until it turned the corner and then got in front of the cab to cut it off and stop it. Jack was out of the passenger side door and the driver of the black car was opening the door in front to talk to the driver.

Jack reached in the back seat and pulled LuLu out. He saw her purse and grabbed it too. She wheeled around on Jack and would have decked him if his reflexes had not been sharper. His hand caught her fist and he propelled her to the back door of the black car, put her inside, and got in next to her. She was furious but before she could yell at him, Jack stared her down and told her, "Not here." She fumed.

The driver had paid the taxi and gotten into the car. He looked in the back seat and Jack nodded to him. The air in the car was tense and heavy. LuLu wanted to yell at him, he wanted to spank her for putting herself in danger, and the driver just wanted to watch the fireworks about to erupt from the back of his car.

They pulled up outside of Jack's building and LuLu had the door open before the car had completely stopped. Jack followed. The doorman just held the door and let them pass. The ride up on the elevator was quiet and the air thick with tension. LuLu waited at the door while Jack opened it. He pushed some security system buttons while LuLu went to her room.

Flo had left at noon so the apartment was empty. Jack followed LuLu to her room and saw her suitcase on the bed. She was packing. That was the last straw!

Jack grabbed her wrist and held her to him. "What do you think you're doing?" Jack growled.

LuLu stopped and tried to pull away. "I'm doing, I'm doing!" her voice rose. "I was taking care of my business and you and your friend came and abducted me! What were <u>you</u> doing?"

She pulled away and went back into the closet. When she came out, he stood in her way. "Look, I was just trying to help out here. I was trying to find out if someone is trying to kill you or kidnap you. You were safe in my apartment, but you had to go off on your own without telling anyone. What was I supposed to do? Oh! You are a damn, exasperating woman!"

She tried to push past him. "Oh, OK, so now what, you want to go? Go where? Oh, Damn it anyway." Jack stormed out of the room.

LuLu put the things on the bed. She was shaking. Ever since Saxby had come to tell them about her pictures on that guys thumb drive, she had been on edge about it and now, now she just wanted to go home. She didn't want anyone taking care of her or watching over her. She just wanted to be left alone.

Jack came back to the door and saw LuLu shaking at the foot of the bed. He walked up behind her and put his arms around her. She turned to face him, tears running down her face. She tried to push away but he held her. Finally, she stopped struggling.

Jack let go of her and asked her to come in the other room with him. She hesitated then followed him.

In the living room he asked her to sit on the sofa, "We need to talk," was all he said. When she had taken a seat, he paced before her.

Jack started off. "Look, I'm sorry for what happened, but we, I was, worried you could be hurt. When I saw you walk out of that service company with that guy and get into the taxi I just had to make sure we got you back where you would be safe. Uh, I, I guess I need to explain."

Jack told her what his friend from MI5 had found out and said the Brits were watching the garage around the clock. When he came back and found her gone, the only place she could have been was the one place they could find with a connection to anything that might be connected to ISIS or any other groups. "Look, I just want you to be safe and maybe I did overreact, but you shouldn't have gone charging in there like you did."

She was listening to him, but looking at her hands and twisting her ring. What he said was right, but it still didn't give him the right to abduct her that way.

He watched her. He hated that he couldn't tell what she was thinking. "LuLu, LuLu," he repeated her name. Finally, she looked up at him. "LuLu, oh damn, I don't' like that name, that is the name of a little girl from the funny papers, I'm calling you Louise. Louise, I just can't have you running all over getting into trouble. Bottom line, listen to me."

Jack went on, "and another thing, look at me when I talk to you. I hate it when you don't pay attention to what I'm saying."

Louise looked at him but not in the way he had expected. Anger flashed in her eyes and she let it out. "Listen to you, listen to you! You're the one that abducted me, pulled me out of the cab, pushed me into that strange car." She was shaking again and this time Jack held her and would not let her go.

When he thought it was safe, he let her sit back down on the sofa. "Look Louise, I promised a lot of people I would look after you and I just want you to let me do that."

This time when she looked at him, the anger was gone. "Do you want to know what I found out or would you rather retrace my steps and check to make sure I am right?"

Jack nodded. Before he let her go on, he asked her if she wanted some brandy and before she could answer, he had poured some for both of them. He handed her a glass and sat down.

"The man I talked to this morning is Lebanese Orthodox. I recognized the name from when I was in Cyprus. He's actually quite a nice fellow. He offered me some coffee before we talked about the car." Louise went on, "He said the man that does the Bentley work is out of town for a couple of days and would be back on Tuesday. Mr. Khoury has been in the United States for a little over forty years and tries to hire people from Lebanon and Syria that are qualified and from the persecuted Christian minority. The man that does the Bentley work is one of the ones he hired just recently."

Louise took a sip of her drink. "I asked him if he was really qualified to service a car of this vintage and he assured me he had the best recommendations. I asked if I could see them and he showed me a letter from the same shop in London that serviced the car for Sir George. I think that is the thing, this guy that services Bentleys is the one you should investigate."

Louise looked rather pleased with herself. She took another sip of brandy and put her glass down. "When this guy gets there on Tuesday, send your "friends" in to talk to him."

Jack was thinking this was probably the case, "but you let me handle it, I don't want you anywhere near there. You were lucky; it may not turn out so good the next time." He was on his feet again. He took his cell phone out and dialed. Within seconds he was talking to someone about what Louise had told him. When he finished, he put the phone down.

Before he could sit down again she was on her feet. "I have some packing to do." She walked out.

Jack followed her down the hall. Damn she was exasperating! His first inclination in the car was to spank her and maybe that is what she needed!

At the room door he didn't knock or ask to come in, he just opened the door and found her putting things in her suitcase. He grabbed her hand and swung her around. He sat on the end of the bed and pulled her across his knee.

She kicked and squirmed but he held her with one arm and brought the other hand down on her butt with a loud whack. The shock of what happened stilled her for a split second then she began to kick and yell.

"Yell all you want Louise, nobody will hear you. This is something you have been needing for a long time and I'm just the one to do it!" The fabric from her skirt was getting in his way and he pulled it up. He wasn't prepared to find her naked ass. Now he spanked her with an open hand that made a loud smack as it landed.

This wasn't turning out the way he had planned. He could feel himself becoming aroused and Louise was no longer yelling at him to stop but wiggling in his lap. He realized the punishment he thought he was dishing out to her had become very erotic play. He stopped and picked her up. The suitcase could wait until later.

CHAPTER 9

Jack reached over Louise's sleeping form. The phone was on vibrate, but he still worried it might wake her up. He slipped out of bed and headed to his bathroom.

The men that had been watching the mechanics apartment had just reported his return. Jack checked his watch and told the men he would be there within the hour. He took care of his business in the bathroom and went back into the bedroom.

Louise was half sitting, the blanket from the bed was covering her lap and her naked breasts with the large dark nipples beckoned him back to bed. He knew he had to go, but he needed to tell her the news first. "Louise, I have to go, the mechanic just got back to his apartment and well, just stay here and I'll be back before you know it." He reached out and caressed her breast and kissed her. She melted into him and her hand caressed his naked cock.

"Mmm, are you sure you need to go?" Jack needed all his will power to pull away from her. He put some clothes on, kissed her, and left.

"Just uh, just don't move and I'll be back." He left the room.

Louise looked around at the large room that was Jack's master bedroom. They had moved up here on Saturday evening or Sunday morning, she couldn't remember which, and only left the room for short times for food. The rest of time they stayed in bed and talked and "got to know" each other.

Now it was Monday evening and the man they wanted to talk to was just getting home. Her car was being off-loaded in the morning and Jack had recommended they wait to pick up the guy when the car got there. The men at the local FBI office were still debating that one.

Louise slipped out of bed and found her cell phone. She was supposed to arrive at the beach house tomorrow evening, but if this was not wrapped up before then, well, then she didn't know. She put her caftan on, and took the stairs down to the kitchen. She wanted to see if there was any food left so she could make dinner.

One of the things about living in New York was the plethora of take-out, to-go, and delivery eateries there were. Anything from deli to gourmet was just a phone call away. Jack was more the meat-and-potatoes kind of guy, much like her father had been, which made ordering for him easy. This time, though, she didn't know how long he would be.

She found a diet soda in the fridge and took it out to the terrace. It was beautiful, but she liked Texas or the beach house. She didn't know what was going to happen, well, not about the bad guys, she knew Jack would take care of them, no, she didn't know what was going to happen between Jack and her.

They had talked or really, he had done most of the talking, but they knew each other better now. Much like Mark had done when they first met; he explained who he was, what he wanted in life, and how she might fit into that life. He had also questioned her about what she would need and want from a relationship. The fine Master/slave negotiation had begun.

Jack had broken through her widowhood. She had spent the last five years carefully keeping herself as Mark had left her and before that, she had kept herself waiting for him to wake up. Now that was all broken. She didn't know what she would do and Jack had given her no indication about anything; only hours of probing talk and wonderful sex.

She finished the soda and started back to the kitchen. There was enough light from the buildings outside that she didn't need to put any on to find her way. About halfway across the room she heard a noise in the hall and froze. She took the soda bottle and tuned it so the neck of the bottle was in her hand and the large glass bottom could be used like a club. The light in the hall came on and Jack was standing at the living room door.

"I thought you weren't going to try and hit me anymore! What did I do now?" He was laughing at her and she joined in. He took the bottle from her and put some bags in the kitchen. While he unpacked the food he had brought he told her what had happened.

The mechanic had come back from wherever he had been and stayed in his apartment for only a few moments before going out. From the way Jack talked, the FBI must have put some listening devices in his apartment before he had returned. They also had some other surveillance on him and were sure he was dirty.

Jack went on. "He walked down the street to a local mosque and stayed there for about half an hour. Problem was, there were no prayer services while he was there. He was meeting someone."

Louise broke in, "that isn't the only problem, Mr. Khoury said he was supposed to be Christian, what is he doing in a mosque?"

Jack nodded, "Exactly. Since your car is supposed to be offloaded tomorrow, they are going to keep him and the car under surveillance until they find out what this guy is up to." He put some plates on the table in the kitchen and they sat down to eat.

Jack reached over and squeezed her hand. "Don't worry, it will all be over soon. We expect them to call and tell you the car has gotten to the shop and this guy is the one that has been sent here to try and harm you. I am not going to let that happen. I will be with you from now until it's over and this guy is behind bars. You know they still have some room down in Gitmo and anybody that tries to hurt you should rot there."

Louise looked down. "And after he is behind bars? What then?"

Jack reached over and put his finger under her chin. "Look at me Louise. What do you want?" She looked at him and tears started to form in her eyes. He could take a lot, but not her tears. "Oh, damn woman, stop crying!" He took a tissue from the box on the counter.

"Louise, there are some things I don't like and one of them is using another man's slave. As long as you wear that collar, you belong to someone else. We both know he is dead, but until you take that off, Mark will always be between us." There he'd said it. She had to understand, he did not want a one-night stand or a weekend fling, he was getting too old for that. He wanted to have the kind of life he felt he should have with the kind of woman that would understand him. Louise was the closest thing he had found since his Emily had passed away.

Jack went on, "I know what I want and that's you, but, well, we both know it is not enough to just wish it or order it. If you want this, a life with me, as my girl, it will mean a lot of work. You need to decide if it's for you."

Jack waited for her to respond. He saw her finger the collar on her neck. He had watched her do that when she was thinking or tired, it was not a conscious habit, but a habit nonetheless.

Louise got up and left the room without a word. Jack felt deflated. He was afraid this might happen. He started taking the dirty dishes off the table and had just put the leftovers in the fridge when Louise came back into the room. She looked at Jack and held out her hand.

When he tried to take her hand, she opened it and saw she was holding a key. He took it from her and she sat down in front of him, lifted her face so her neck was exposed. She lifted the flap that covered the lock that kept the collar around her neck. Jack sat down in the chair in front of her and put the key in the lock and opened it. The collar fell onto her shoulders and she took it in her hands. For the first time since Mark had put it on her, she was without it.

She took the key back from Jack, put it with the collar, and put them both on the table. Jack pulled her to him and whispered in her ear, "Stay with me Louise, stay with me and let me play with you, love you, care for you, protect you." He could feel the tears falling on his shoulder again, but this time, he was sure they were happy tears.

He stood her up, "come here, I have something I want to show you." He walked her back up the stairs to his suite. He opened the door to the closet and walked to the back. A small panel was barely visible but popped open when he pushed it. It was a door.

Jack went in first and Louise heard the faint click of a light switch. Jack took Louise by the hand and pulled her inside. Behind the closet was another room, a dungeon. The walls were a dark green and the furniture was sparse but adequate for a private play area.

"When I bought this apartment, it had been in the same hands since before the war when this building was built so it needed a lot of renovations. All I needed up on this floor was a bedroom and office, there are two bedrooms on the floor you're on, so the extra space was put back here as a private playroom for when Emily and I were in New

York. Only two problems; all of the stuff in here had to be built inside the room and Emily hated New York so she and I never used it."

"I have tried using it with people from time to time, but it was all very, uhm, unsatisfying." He turned to look at Louise. "I know we have not negotiated play rules between us yet, but do you trust me Louise? Do you trust me enough to let me play with you?"

Louise thought for a moment. So there it was, the test. All these years she had relived that night at the Social Club when Mark had his stroke and hurt her. Could she ever trust or not?

Jack saw the turmoil in her eyes. "Louise, I am not Mark and this is not the same. If you need to safeword, it's ok, it means I am not reading your body right and there is nothing I want to learn more than to read you. Do you trust me?" All he could do now was wait for her to make a move.

He saw her eyes go to the spanking bench. She nodded, "Yes, I trust you." He pulled her to him and kissed her. She felt so good in his arms, it was time to see if the other part of their life would be as fulfilling, for both of them.

She let her caftan fall to the floor, then picked it up and put it on a chair near the bench. She was naked except for her sandals and she kicked those to the side. Jack looked at her. She was the same age as he was so he knew that she would be no tight-skinned newbie with high perky breasts, but a woman in the full sense of the word. To him she was beautiful and just perfect.

He went to his toy chest and pulled a pair of cuffs out for her wrists and another pair for her ankles. He laid them out along with some other toys and started to put them on her. She helped with the wrist and ankle cuffs. He then brought a heavy leather collar that he had used before. She looked at it and then into his eyes. "It's only for play," he told her and she pulled her hair back while he put it on.

He led her to the spanking bench and she laid down across it. He fastened her ankles and wrists to the eyebolts and then the collar secured to the end of the bench. The last thing was the blindfold. He leaned down and kissed her; then the music began to play.

The sound masked the other movements he made around the small room. He took a pair of floggers from the toy box, a galley-whip, and a braided riding crop. He also had a paddle, but didn't know if he would use it, perhaps this would be enough for the first time.

Louise had had plenty of time to think about what he was doing, it was the anticipation of what was to come, the not knowing that added to the experience. The music was on a loop and would continue to cycle for as long as he wanted it to, but now it was time to start.

He rubbed his hands over her body. The pale skin was warm to his touch, down her back he moved slowly, purposefully. Finally, her exposed ass-cheeks, just a hint of the spanking he had given her the other night still showing on her fair skin. He rubbed her thighs, her hips, her inner thighs, he was becoming familiar with her anatomy and what he saw he liked. She was perfect for him. Now it was time to see if he would be right for her.

He moved his hand higher and felt the outer lips of her pussy and felt her push against him. With one finger, he tested her and found her wet and wanting. He knew he wanted her, but not just yet, first they needed some play. His open hand smacked against her skin and she pulled against the restraints. Again he smacked her, this time in a different spot and she bucked again, a third time, but now she was starting to relax into the spanking. She was beginning to feel him and trust him.

He continued to smack her in time to the music and each time she would push into his strike. Every few smacks he would caress her ass and it was getting redder and redder. He moved to the side and let her feel his weight against her body, she pushed toward him.

The music changed to a different beat and he picked up his flogger, a doe hide soft one that would be wonderful to warm-up with. He put his mouth next to her ear and told her she was a good girl and he was proud of her, he asked her if she wanted him to continue. She nodded. He took a couple of practice swings with the flogger and the soft falls made a whooshing sound as they cut the air.

He started on her back and then each side of her hips. By the time he got to her ass, she knew what was coming and rose against the restraints to meet the falls as they hit her. After several more minutes he took the braided riding crop and moved it over her back, down her sides, across her ass cheeks and then to her inner thighs. He took the tip and moved it toward her pussy, but then pulled it back. He knew she could probably cum if he continued, but it wasn't time for that yet.

He brought the crop down on her back in a soft, controlled manner and kept it like that until he knew she was not afraid. He would hit her with it then caress her until he was leaving small welts on her backside. So far, she had not cried out or done more than move against the restraints. Now, though, she was pulling away more than she was pushing into the crop. He wondered if he should go on, but when he whispered to her she told him to continue.

Jack laid the crop down and picked up the galley-whip. This would give her more of a stingy sensation than "thuddy" and he worried it might be too much for her, but he wanted to try. The music continued to grow and with it his need to really use her and possess her. Now it was Jack who was driving the session and Louise felt it. When he leaned against her, she could feel his hard cock press against her. When he whispered in her ear, she could hear his desire and need and she begged him to take her.

Jack had put the toys down, now his hands traveled over her body and he could feel the rising welts he had put there. His hands caressed her thighs and his fingers parted her pussy-lips and found her so very, very wet. Jack unzipped his pants and took out his cock, he moved to her head and pulling a hand-full of her hair up, raised her head, her mouth open, and he put his cock in her mouth. He moved his hips as she sucked his head and flicked it with her tongue, he didn't want to cum like this, but he was so close, he pulled his cock out and let her head rest where it had been before.

Now he moved to the back and the design of the bench let him get in exactly the right spot. He slid his cock into her pussy and then, slowly at first, then with more force, keeping in time to the music, he pushed deeper and deeper into her. She pushed back against him, she wanted this and couldn't get enough of him.

Quietly at first, and then louder, she heard herself over the music begging him to let her cum, pleading with him to let her orgasm. Finally, it reached through the music to Jack's ears and he realized that she would never cum without his permission. Just as he was about to push his load into her he growled at her to cum, to give him his prize, yes, he wanted her to cum for him.

The two of them exploded around each other, and then stilled, the music started to fade. Exhausted, he undid first the collar, then the ankle restraints and finally her wrists. She took the blindfold off and laid it on the bench. He sat on the chair next to the spanking bench and held her and rocked her, and stroked her hair. Nothing was said, nothing needed to be said.

CHAPTER 10

Just before dawn, Jack and Louise were sitting in the kitchen drinking coffee; it was Tuesday. The play from the night before had worn them both out, but the adrenalin pumping in them over the mechanic would not let them rest. Today they hoped to find out what the threat was from and how to deal with it.

Jack had put his foot down and told Louise she could not go and stake out the garage with them. Normally that would have guaranteed that she would go, but she knew Jack was only doing what was best for her and besides, she trusted him. If there was any time to show how much she trusted him, this was it.

Flo had just come in and offered to make them breakfast, but Jack declined and Louise couldn't eat until Jack got back and she knew he was safe. Flo watched the way they kissed goodbye and figured there was now a permanent woman in Jack's life. That was good, men got into too much "no good" when they were alone all the time.

Louise stayed in the kitchen with Flo and watched her while she cooked. The two women sat at the table and drank coffee, waiting for word to come. Flo told Louise about life in Jamaica when she was a little girl, before her family brought her to New York, and Louise told her about Texas and growing up in Houston.

A pot of coffee later and the phone was still silent. By ten in the morning, Flo could see Louise was very worried. At five past eleven, the phone next to Louise rang; it was Jack's number. The call was brief, but Louise let out a big sigh as she hung up the phone.

Then the tears started. She didn't realize she had been this stressed over the mechanic, but the release of tension simply deflated her and she started sobbing.

Flo handed her the box of tissues and Louise had just stopped crying when Jack walked back into the apartment. That started the tears over again.

Jack had an FBI agent with him, the same man that had been the driver of the black car the past Saturday when she had gone to the garage. He waited until Louise calmed down. Flo plied him with coffee and cake while he waited.

They sat in the living room while the man asked her some questions and she asked some of her own. He showed her a picture of the man they all called the mechanic, but, no, she did not recognize him. Next came a picture of the two brothers that owned the shop in London and no, the only contact had been by phone and no, they just sounded like regular Brits.

Finally, the man thanked her, shook hands with Jack, and said goodbye to Flo on his way out. Jack gave Flo the rest of the day off and when she was gone, brought some champagne into the living room with two glasses.

He looked around but Louise was not there. He saw the door to the second floor open and climbed the stairs.

Louise was sitting in bed, waiting for Jack. He put the bottle of bubbly and the glasses on the dresser and joined her. The champagne would wait.

Later, much later, he finally explained all the details. It wasn't her they wanted, but the car. The brother in London had loaded some explosives in the car in places most customs searches would not look. A liberal sprinkling of garlic oil on the undercarriage would throw off the dogs trained to sniff out explosives. Before the car would be delivered to the garage in New York, the mechanic was supposed to make a stop at a rental unit, take out the explosives, and go on to the garage and put the car back together so no one would be the wiser. The explosives were to be used by another group against some targets in New York; the tunnel or one of the busy bridges being high on their list. The FBI nabbed more than one operative that morning, and it was all because of her picture being on the thumb drive in London.

EPILOGUE

Louise, Lady Margaret, and Harry stood in the dungeon vault before the glass case that held the brands of the club's members. One of the officers of the club opened the case, removed the dragon brand of Mark, and handed it to Harry. Louise had asked Harry, as a close friend, to do the honors and lay Mark, forever, to rest.

With a diamond tipped blade, Harry defaced the brand so it would never again be used. Next, he tied a black ribbon around the leather binder that held the contract and placed it back on the shelf in the case. He put the damaged brand on top and around it, the collar Louise had worn as Mark's slave. The officer locked the case. Master Mark would always be honored as a past Master but for Louise, life could now go on.

Earlier in the day, Harry had stood with his friend, Jack, as the other Masters formally accepted him as a member of the group. Louise and Maggie left the vault to be taken back to the house before the other men celebrated the addition of the new member. Tonight there would only be the Masters in the club to celebrate.

The following day, Maggie and Louise were standing just beyond the circle of light coming from the center of the dungeon. The group of Masters stood in their best dress leathers or in formal attire. Before them, on cushions, their respective slaves knelt in a formal kneel. Each slave held a candle with the electric flame turned to the lowest level. Two slave girls, dressed in transparent black robes, came to the edge of the darkness and led Margaret and Louise to the stage in the center of the room.

Standing on the stage, Jack and Harry were waiting for them. Maggie knelt in front of Harry and Louise in front of Jack. One of the Masters brought in a pillow with a velvet bag lying on it. Jack took the bag, removed its contents, and handed the empty bag to Harry. In Jack's hand was a beautiful collar, made especially for Louise. The clasp was a wolf's head and the body was made of braided strands of platinum metal, the eyes of the wolf were diamonds.

Jack looked down at Louise and she looked up at him. In a clear, strong voice, Jack asked Louise to repeat her name. "Louise Harris, Sir." After a few seconds, he asked her why she was there, "IF you will have me, I am here to offer myself to you in service, body, behavior, and attitude; to be your property, to obey and serve you, to make your life easier and more peaceful. I will give you my advice when asked and use my talents when needed. To care for you when you are sick, laugh with you when you are happy, and cry with you when you are sad. I give myself to you totally. I want to follow you wherever you will lead. This I say with a solemn vow."

Jack reached down to attach the collar around her neck. He pulled her up to him and kissed her long and hard. The group around them clapped. Next, he attached her to the chain that hung down from the ceiling and the eyebolts in the floor.

The blindfold and ball gag were provided by Maggie. Harry helped Jack with his brand. For fourteen seconds the cold block burned the wolf symbol into her skin and Louise's muffled screams were heard from behind the gag. When it was removed, she showed off her new brand, and for the first time since they had joined, changed the "Sir" to "Master", signifying her position as his slave.

Tenderly, Jack took his newly collared slave/wife down, lovingly kissed her, and stroked her hair. She melted in his embrace as he leaned his head back, and gave a wolf's cry that split the air. There would still be a reading of the contract and the party to follow, but today he was the happiest man alive. Master Jack and slave Louise, the Grey Wolf and his mate.